PRAISE

MW00328088

"Vivian Arend does a wonderful job of building the atmosphere and the other characters in this story so that readers will be sucked into the world and looking forward to the rest of the books in the series."
~ *Library Journal*

"Steamy and sweet complete with a whole host of colourful side characters and enough sub-plots to get your teeth into. A fab read!"
~ *Scorching Book Reviews*

"There's a real chemistry between the characters, laced with humor and snappy dialogue and no shortage of steamy sex scenes to keep things lively. The result is an entertaining, spicy romance."
~ *Publishers Weekly*

Silver Mine is an outstanding story. The author creates a world that invites readers for the ride of their lives."
~ *Coffee Time Romance Reviews*

Arend offers constant action and thrills, and her characters are so captivating and nuanced that readers will have a hard time guessing who the villains really are.
~ *RT Book Reviews*

A full list of Vivian's print titles is available on her website

www.vivianarend.com

WOLF SIGNS

NORTHERN LIGHTS EDITION

VIVIAN AREND

This is a work of fiction. Names, characters, places, and incidents either are the product of the author's imagination or are used fictitiously, and any resemblance to any persons, living or dead, business establishments, events, or locales is entirely coincidental.

Wolf Signs
Copyright © 2009 by Arend Publishing Inc.
ISBN: 9781989507780
Edited by Anne Scott
Cover Design by Croco Designs
Proofed by Sharon Muha

All rights reserved. No part of this book may be used or reproduced in any manner whatsoever without written permission except in the case of brief quotations.

To My Sweetie,
We haven't quite traveled the world but we're on our way.
Thanks for finding some awesome settings for us to explore.
I'd like to write a couple of African adventures and maybe
something set in New Zealand. You up for it? I love research.

*6*450 calories stared up at Robyn.

She adjusted the lid on the apple box, closing it tightly over the cheesecake and the rest of her food supplies. Her gaze drifted over the gear spread all over her apartment. Her pack, her skis—all of it assembled for the annual trip with her brother to Granite Lake cabin.

A rush of anxiety and disappointment filled her as Tad made his announcement.

"I'm sorry, sis, but I have to take this request. Flying the climbing and research team to Mount Logan could end up being a regular booking. They'll be working in Kluane National Park for the next five years, and if I can get on as their main pilot I'll be set." Tad slipped a loose strand of hair behind her ear. "I hate to cancel the trip on you."

Robyn paced a few steps away before facing him, her hands flowing smoothly as she spoke in American Sign Language. "I understand. You need to take the job. I'm still going to Granite Lake."

"No way. You can't go by yourself."

"You have."

"But that's different, Robyn."

"Don't be a jerk. I don't have a penis so I can't go backcountry alone?"

Tad raised a brow. "It's not the lack of plumbing, sis, and you know it. I seldom go bush alone, and if I do meet anyone, it's not a big deal. I'm male, I'm strong and I'm not deaf. How do you plan to talk with strangers?"

She threw a pillow at him before lifting her hands to sign. "I'll take some notepads. What are the chances of meeting anyone at Granite this time of year? We always go in February because no one else does. I'm packed, the food is packed, and I've got time off work from the bakery. You even booked a helicopter ride for me with your buddy Shaun. I've never gotten to fly in before.

"And wait a minute, what's with that little dig saying *you're* strong? Last time I checked, I out-skied, out-wrestled and out-gambled your sorry butt, big brother. Don't give me that as an excuse."

Tad narrowed his gaze. "Stop being stubborn."

"What? Waste all those years of training? You told me once to stand up for myself and do what I need to do, in spite of not being able to hear. Are you saying that doesn't apply anymore?"

"Of course not—"

"Good, because I'd hate to call you a hypocrite." Annoyance aside, she really needed him to understand. "I need to go to Granite. I need to get out of the city for a while. I'll be a good little girl and take the satellite phone along. I can check in with you Tuesday."

Tad ran a hand through his hair before collapsing on the couch in resignation. "Fine, you win. But if you need anything you call me, or you call Shaun and he'll fly you home. Understand? You don't have to do the ski out if you don't want."

Robyn caught a glimpse of herself in the hall mirror. Shades of brown reflected back. Shoulder-length brown hair, big brown eyes with golden flecks, skin that showed her First Nations heritage.

She'd lived her whole life in the Yukon, and her solid body was more than capable of doing the ten-mile ski. She'd been completing it with the family since she was nine years old. Tad had skied the route with her and knew she loved every minute of the trip.

She counted to twenty.

Slowly.

"Tad, are you looking for pain? Because I can kick your butt if you need it."

He blinked in shock. "What did I say?"

Robyn stomped up and glared in his face. Tad was her brother through adoption, and he and his parents were all darker in colouring than her. His short black hair stood in ragged spikes from his manhandling, and his dark eyes stared back with confusion.

She needed to make this clear, though. She signed, hands moving with great energy as she emphasized her points. "I *like* the ski across the lake. I *like* going to the Granite Lake cabin. I'm thrilled you got me the helicopter ride, but only because I want to take the ice auger to leave at the cabin."

"But—"

"Don't expect me to be some kind of baby because you can't go with me this time."

Tad grabbed her hands and pulled her in for a hug. He let her step back so she could read his lips. "I was out of line."

She nodded.

"Sorry. Hell, you've got a temper on you. Glad you didn't throw anything hard at me this time."

"I thought about it but my ice axe is already packed." She turned to tuck away a few more items, then grabbed her backpack and placed it beside the door.

He tugged on her arm to get her attention. "You need some space, don't you? You seem really tense."

Robyn returned to her skis. She fiddled with the bindings before glancing back at Tad. "Yeah. Feels like the walls are closing in. I'll be okay if I can get some time away from the city."

"There's something..." Tad hesitated, looking everywhere around the room except at her. He opened and closed his mouth a couple of times before shaking his head. "Never mind."

She sighed heavily. "Not again. You do this at least once a year. Whatever deep, dark secret you have, I wish you'd spit it out. Or stop bringing it up, because you just get me curious. Are you gay?"

Tad sat back on his heels, his jaw dropping open. "Robyn!"

"Well, you seem to turn twenty shades of red every time you start this, I thought maybe it had to do with sex. I don't care if you are gay, you know. There's this great guy down at the bakery—"

"Thanks, but I'm not gay. It's nothing. Do you have your bear spray?"

She blew her bangs off her face with a sudden snort and pointed to the pocket of her ski overalls. "Stupidest thing I've ever carried. I've never seen a bear, not once in all our trips."

"Someday you might be glad you have it, sis."

"But I could carry at least five more chocolate bars. That reminds me, you do realize if I gain weight this trip it's all your fault."

"What?"

"We packed an entire Mocha Chocolate Cheesecake to eat this week. Now I'm going to have to suffer through and eat the whole damn thing myself." She licked her lips and grinned.

~

THE PILOT TUGGED on her sleeve and pointed twice—first left toward the lake then farther to the right behind the cabin.

She shook her head and picked the left.

The lake.

The helicopter banked as he veered to change course. The surface snow around them stirred under the effects of the spinning props, and whiteness whirled away from the chopper until there was nothing but the solid snow base under the landing gear.

Robyn waited while the pilot trotted around to open her door. She helped unhook her skis from the landing blades while he removed the rest of her gear from the backseat and dropped it on the snow beside them. In under a minute she'd done a final check to be sure all her things were out, then giving the pilot a thumb's up, she crouched low and scrambled toward the shoreline. The wind buffeted her for a minute as the helicopter rose, lifting over the small hill to the north, returning to Haines Junction.

She looked around her and drew a long, slow breath, crisp air chilling the back of her throat. Not a cloud in the sky to block the blue. The mountains around her tall and snow covered. Beautiful and overpowering at the same time. The lake spread before her, its large bay at her feet and the longer length of it stretching snakelike to the south to disappear around the bend of the mountain. A sense of home spread throughout her body.

Twisting in a circle, she noticed the cabin facing the lake had been fixed up since the last time she'd been out. Someone had repaired the front-porch supports and added a series of hooks along the north wall. Snow shovels and axes that had been buried under a good four feet of snow last February hung in plain sight, easy to access.

Continuing her visual scan, Robyn was surprised to see a new building a little ways from the cabin. It was too small to be another sleeping area, and they didn't need any more storage.

The temperature was warm for February, twenty-seven degrees, but the chill sank into her bones the longer she stood in one place. She trudged back through her footprints to ferry her gear to the cabin. The new building would be her treat to explore once she got set up for the night.

Soon her backpack rested on the low platform covering the back of the tiny one-room cabin. There was space for six sleeping bags to lie side by side, with an extra three-foot extension at their feet that was used as a bench. Robyn considered for a minute before placing her pack along the sidewall near the window. She doubted anyone else would show up at the cabin, but she'd better stake her claim just in case.

The second trip, she carried up the cardboard apple box filled with groceries. Because of the helicopter, the food this trip was different than her usual dry goods. She had fresh fruit and veggies for at least four days, some nice French loaves, and the dreaded Mocha Chocolate Cheesecake. Flying in had some definite fringe benefits.

She left the box on the small counter that ran along the left-hand wall up to the wood-burning stove. The cabin was so compact there was barely room left for a table and four chairs on the right side and a narrow bench beside the solid plank door.

Returning to the lake, she used the ice auger to cut a hole in the ice surface before carrying the tool to the cabin and finding an empty hook to hang it on. Robyn grinned as she stared at it for a minute. She'd bought her contribution to the "leave it better than you found it" policy in a garage sale the previous summer for twenty bucks.

Lake trout for dinner. She could hardly wait.

But first she would check out the new addition to the area.

Making her way through the knee-deep snow, she climbed the last couple of steps that rose above the snow line, undid the locks and peeked in.

There was a small open area with two side windows and a snow-covered skylight overhead. Wood dowels lined the interior walls at head height with a low bench running around the wall space. Another door was set in the center of room.

Good heavens, was that a shower in the corner? Robyn walked to the enclosure in amazement. Someone had brought a shower stall to Granite Lake and installed it in this small cabin.

Her heart leapt for a second, wondering if her guess of what was in the other room was correct.

She hurried back, opened the central door and walked into the smell of cedar and wood smoke. In the corner was an old potbellied stove with river rocks piled all around it.

Two levels of benches were built into the walls and a couple of large buckets graced the top of the stove.

A sauna. Someone had built a sauna. She'd died and gone to heaven.

Tad was going to be pissed he'd missed this.

But the real debate became whether she wanted get the fire going, or if she should still go fishing for her dinner.

Robyn ran her hand over the smooth wood and breathed in the rich scent. Actually, it was an easy decision. She'd do both. Getting the fire going wasn't a big deal, and she'd have time to fish before it warmed up properly.

The next hours passed quickly while she set up her fishing line, laid out her camping mattress and sleeping bag, and got the two stoves going.

By six it was dark and she lay flat on her back on one of the upper benches in the now-toasty sauna. She'd enjoyed pan-fried trout for dinner along with a glass of merlot, and she was on the edge of feeling very, very good. Her frustrations slipped away with the sweat pouring off her body.

This was roughing it.

She sat up, scooped some more of the melting snow from the pot on the stove and poured it with care over the hot rocks to build up the steam in the room. Noticing the pot was close to empty she slipped into the annex and pulled on her boots. Propping open the outside door, she walked into the darkness with a bucket in either hand.

And slammed into something solid that hadn't been there before. Something tall and hard and covered in...Gore-Tex?

2

TJ froze in shock for a second as a naked woman bounced off him and fell backward, metal buckets flying from her hands. He reached to catch her before she could hit the snow, speaking calmly as she struggled in his arms.

"Whoa now, settle down. Sorry, didn't mean to surprise you."

She continued to twist and scramble, one hand reaching toward her boots. He would have released her, but was afraid with how much she was squirming she would hurt herself.

A sharp jab in the ribs made him gasp and loosen his grip. Another blow landed closer to his groin and his hands grew looser still.

"TJ, let her go, she's freaking out," Keil called from a short distance away and distracted, TJ dropped her.

Oh, damn.

"What the...? Hey, put that away, you little hellion. I told you I'm not going to hurt you." He stepped away from where the woman crouched, a fixed-blade hunting knife extended between them as she scurried back toward the safety of the sauna house. She slammed the door followed immediately by the shriek of something heavy being dragged in front of it.

"What is going on? Hey, lady, we're not going to hurt you. We're just—"

"Stop." Keil joined him at the door. "There's something happening here that isn't normal. We surprised her, but something else is wrong." He lifted his hand to touch the wooden barrier, then leaned forward and sniffed a couple of times, concern drawing his face tight.

TJ stopped as well and sniffed the air. "Shit, she's a wolf." He shook his head in frustration. "Try and get away from pack for a few days, and look what happens. It's like a conspiracy. Do you think that someone out there has a spy camera keeping track of us when we leave Haines? That would be kinda cool if it was a hot group, you know, like the KGB, FBI, CSI, SEALs and all those letter guys. But not the SPCA or PETA—it would be scary having *them* on our ass."

He shuffled over to where his brother was concentrating hard. Keil had leaned his forehead against the door and closed his eyes while continuing to draw long, slow breaths.

What was making him act so weird? He was like a kid in a candy store. Mr. In Charge, Super Wilderness Man, always totally with it and in control, sniffing like a dog after a long-buried bone.

Something was up, but for the life of him TJ couldn't figure out what.

TJ sniffed again, hard, before shrugging. He turned away, hitting his brother's arm as he moved, letting a wicked chuckle escape. "Of course, she was rather sweet. Think she'd be interested in—"

A violent push sent him flying backward into the snow.

"Hey, watch it!" He sat up in the waist-deep snow and brushed off his hands, muttering insults at his big brother. "Man, your sense of humour is in a knot tonight. You need to lighten up..."

A low, menacing growl made him pause from his fussing. Keil stalked toward him, eyes dark, teeth showing.

The hair on the back of TJ's neck went erect, and he scrambled backward through the thick snow, trying to keep a safe distance between them.

"Damn it, what is *wrong* with you? I was joking around."

Keil paused. He dropped his head, and his body shook as he took deep, calming breaths. Long heartbeats later he reached to help pull TJ to his feet.

They stared at each other before Keil turned back toward the sauna.

"Ummm, bro, what's up?" TJ asked cautiously. "You look a little grey around the edges and that's not like you. I mean, there's a chick here. It won't be the quiet getaway we planned, but it's not like we ran into an Elvis-impersonator reunion. She's not going to be any trouble."

Keil choked out a laugh, a brittle, tight sound that made TJ take a cautionary step farther out of reach.

Just in case.

Finally dragging his gaze off the sauna door, his brother gave TJ a soft push on the shoulder toward the cabin. "We're going to have to write her a note or something to convince her it's safe to come out."

"Why don't we let her stay in there until the morning? She might feel safer venturing out in the daylight," TJ suggested as he started up the path.

"I'm not leaving her locked in there!"

"Hey, don't bite my head off. I wasn't the one streaking in the moonlight. This time. And the only time I did try it, those rotten twins, Rachel and Beth, stole my clothes and I had to climb in the back window of the pack house..." TJ's voice trickled away to nothing as he realized his brother was still standing by the sauna door. Shaking his head, he called in a singsong voice, "Helloooo. Earth to Keil. Hey, I thought we were going to write a note. What is the matter with you, man? You're acting like you've never seen a woman before, and that's not true. You have the chicks all over you, all the time. In the pack and out of it. Not that you take advantage of your opportunities like I think you should. Leave her alone. She'll be fine. It's not like she's going to freeze or anything."

A loud snort followed him. "Look," Keil said, "I'm not leaving my mate locked in a sauna all night because I was too stupid to figure out how to fix a misunderstanding."

TJ stopped in midstride. "Your mate?"

Keil sighed, his head turning to the sauna as if drawn to it. "Yup. I think so."

"Oh shit."

ROBYN PEERED out the window until the two men left. They disappeared from sight, and candlelight appeared in the windows of the cabin.

Well, that had been just peachy.

Great going. Way to use your brains.

What a stupid, idiotic thing to do—walk outside in the buff without checking around first. She knew better than to assume people wouldn't show up. She hadn't even thought about animals, although right now she wished she had wandered into a bear.

This was the kind of accident Tad had warned her about. Why he didn't like it when she did trips without him or their core group of friends. She was capable of taking care of herself in a survivor-type situation, but adding people to the mix always made it tough. The fact she was deaf kind of guaranteed when meeting new people in the wilderness, something was going to go screwy.

She dropped back on the sauna bench and tried to relax. She was still holding her knife, and twisting the handle in her palm, she rubbed the carvings with her fingertips like a worry stone. Over and over until the familiar sensation calmed her to the point she could begin to see the humour in the situation.

I bet they never expected to get flashed. She poured some of the now-hot water over her skin, cleaning off the sweat and rinsing her hair. She wondered if the men would want the sauna once she was done. She wouldn't stock the stove, but leave a bed of coals.

Because she had to go back inside the main cabin. It would be monumentally silly to spend the night in the sauna just because she'd had a bit of a shock.

Besides, now they knew she had a big knife.

She toweled off in the sauna then stepped into the annex to get dressed. A piece of white against the window caught her eye, and she lifted a candle to examine it.

So sorry we frightened you. We're Keil and TJ from Haines, Alaska, and operate the wilderness excursion company Maximum Exposure. We're members of the Granite Lake pack.

*If you're afraid to come to the cabin, please put two lit
candles in the window, and we'll bring your sleeping gear
and food/water to the door, and you can retrieve it when you
feel safe. But we promise you're safe to return.*

If you want, approach in wolf.

Robyn read the note with some puzzlement. Well, the
first part was nice, but what were they talking about
"approach in wolf"?

Must be some kind of backcountry code she hadn't
picked up yet. They were from Haines—maybe it was an
American slang. Sometimes the small differences between
American and Canadian vocabularies caused weird things
to happen.

She hung her wet towel in the sauna, then wrapped her
hair in a dry one and faced the door. Squaring her
shoulders, she drew a deep breath. She could do this.

Walking toward the cabin, she peered in the window,
checking it out before approaching the door. One of the
men sat on the edge of the sleeping platform, his face out of
sight as he spoke, his hands moving wildly as they swung in
big circles.

Great, a waver. All that energy saying nothing.

The other leaned back against the table, his arms
supporting him, his gaze roaming the room. Suddenly he
looked straight at her out the window. Even though she
should be invisible to him, a person in the dark while he was
in the light, he'd seen her. He stood a little straighter, and
lifting his arms, he crossed them over his heart and dipped
his head.

Robyn stopped in shock.

That was the ASL sign for "love".

Her last straw broke, and she stomped the rest of the way to the cabin and threw open the door. Dropping her things on the bench, she kicked off her boots and marched up to the bastard and started the deaf equivalent of shouting with her hands and body in his personal space.

"You do not insult me like that. Asshole. I accept your apology for the mistake before, but you go too far. You are rude. What does...?" She pulled the paper she'd retrieved from the window and pointed to the line "approach in wolf". "What does this mean?"

She stepped back and crossed her arms while she waited for his response.

The look on his face was priceless.

Confusion. Complete and utter confusion.

Robyn spun toward the waver as he stood, and she caught the last thing he said. "...using sign language?"

She nodded, bicycling her hands in front of her while mouthing "sign language".

The larger of the two men made sure she was watching him before he spoke. "I'm sorry, I don't understand sign language. I think I've upset you, and I didn't mean to. Is there a way we can talk?"

All the bluster drained out of her like sand through a sieve. Typical. She came to get away from the drain of communicating with people, and instead she was going to have to use extra energy.

Oh well, maybe they'd eat a few pieces of her cheesecake and save her the calories.

She held up a hand with a lifted finger—a signal she'd seen many hearing people use to ask for a minute. Going back to the door, she cleaned up her boots before returning to her backpack to tuck away her gear and tidy her hair.

She turned to get a drink and found the man she'd yelled at standing right behind her with a glass in his hand.

"Would you like some water?" He held it toward her.

Robyn touched her fingers to her mouth then opened the hand toward him before accepting the glass. She drained it in one shot, grinning at the funny expression on his face as she returned the glass.

It had been hot in the sauna, and she wasn't going to be ladylike and sip when she was thirsty.

He smiled back. Dark brown eyes, so dark they were almost black, twinkled at her.

"Would you like some more?"

She nodded and made a circle motion over her chest with her hand.

"Was that 'please'?" he asked.

Robyn gave him a reluctant smile. She nodded as she settled at the table.

There was something fascinating about the man, and she watched as he went to get her some more water.

She'd placed snow-filled buckets here in the main cabin before her sauna, and the men knew the routine. They had one of the buckets on the side cupboard for cool water, and the other simmering on the stove to melt snow and keep the air moist.

It was impossible to look away from the man's smoothly flexing muscles as he added more snow to the hot bucket. He was big. One of the biggest men she'd ever seen, and perhaps rushing into the cabin and shouting at him hadn't been the smartest thing to do.

His dark brown hair hung in a braid almost to his hips. Broad shoulders were covered with a dark T-shirt, and a tribal tattoo wrapped around his left arm at the biceps. She was tempted to move closer and examine it, but he returned with her full glass, and she tried to hide the fact she'd been staring by facing the table.

She spotted the notepad and pencil she'd left out earlier. She tapped it and motioned for him to sit beside her.

You talk and I'll write. You need to make sure I see your face.

"I'm Keil and that's my brother, TJ."

Robyn Maxwell from Whitehorse.

"I'm sorry we frightened—"

She interrupted him by waving a hand in the air and writing. *It was an accident. I couldn't hear you and I wasn't paying attention. Tell TJ I'm sorry I pulled my knife on him.*

Keil rotated to face his brother, and a moment later, TJ settled in the chair opposite her and held out his hand. "Nice to meet you, Robyn," he said, drawing out his words in an exaggerated manner.

Oh goodie. TJ was an idiot.

She glared then shook his hand hard enough to make him pull back in surprise. She grabbed the pad.

I'm deaf, not stupid. Don't talk weird for my sake. She flipped the pad around to let him read while she took another drink.

This was the hard way to get to know people. It was much easier when Tad was along, because she could talk to him and he'd pass on messages, and it would end up feeling natural and not this ridiculously slow process.

She sighed and grabbed the pad back.

Keil laid a soft hand on her arm to get her attention, and a curious sensation raced through her.

Heat slid from his hand to her arm, tickling, tingling. She double-checked—it was just his hand, but warmth still radiated, small bursts of electricity racing up her arm and making the hair on the back of her neck stand on end.

He gave a slight squeeze to get her attention, and she glanced at his face.

"What pack?"

She pulled back in confusion and shrugged.

"You said you live in Whitehorse. Are you Takhini or Miles Canyon pack?"

Here they went again. What was he *talking* about?

It was too bad he seemed to be slightly crazy because he was the hottest thing on two legs she'd ever seen. She hoped he was fun crazy and not kill-people-in-the-middle-of-the-night crazy.

It only took a moment to dash down a short note. She tossed the pad toward him as she got up from the table and pulled on her coat.

Robyn took a final quick glance his direction before heading outside for a breath of air. Yup, he was hot. Out of his mind, but very easy on the eyes. Smelt yummy, too.

She ignored the strange throbbing sensation in her limbs and forced herself to walk outside.

As THE DOOR closed behind her, Keil pulled the pad nearer and read it out loud to TJ.

"Takhini is a hot spring. Miles Canyon is where I canoe. A pack is what I carry my gear in. I don't know what you're talking about. I'm getting ready for bed. The sauna has coals if you want it. I will talk to you tomorrow. Good night."

"You think she really doesn't know she's a werewolf?" TJ asked.

"Why would she have any reason to pretend? I don't understand. She's full-blood wolf from what I smell."

"Me too."

Keil drummed his fingers on the table. She not only smelt like wolf, but another scent flowed from her that tickled the back of his brain and went straight to his cock.

The scent of his mate. The chemical trail that called his wolf to hers, and would make them mates for life. He was pretty sure she was it, but until he got a taste of her when she was aroused, he couldn't be positive.

Of course, at the rate they were going, it would be summer before he'd get close enough to actually find out.

Grabbing clean clothes, the brothers made their way to the sauna.

Not even ten seconds after closing the door, Keil realized the sauna was a bad idea. Her scent hung heavy in the air, sweet and spicy, filling his head with thoughts that were better not imagined while sitting naked in a small space with someone who was not her.

"You know, she smells good."

Keil growled at TJ. "Shut it, pup."

His brother shrugged. "Well, she does. But she smells good like 'Hey, Robyn, can you help me with this?' and not 'Hey, baby, can you help me? Wink, wink, nudge, nudge.' Know what I mean?"

"Please, spare me the Monty Python imitations."

TJ flicked some snow at his brother. "I'm trying to tell you something serious and you accuse me of imitating MP? I'm cut to the quick. For serious discussion I imitate political personalities."

Keil lay back on the bench and attempted to ignore his younger brother. TJ was the most irritating, the most annoying...and one of the most observant people he knew.

Leaning up on one elbow, he opened his eyes and cursed. "Fine. Explain it. What're you trying to tell me, and use small words. It's late, and it's been a hell of a day."

TJ dropped to the lower bench and grabbed the cedar edging in front of him. "She smells good like I want to trust her and take care of her, and I know she'll take care of me. She *obviously* affects you differently."

"Oh. How is that?"

TJ snorted. "You've got wood just from the smell of her, bro. You've got it bad, and I bet she's your mate because you haven't even given her a proper sniff yet. I knew you were ready to be Alpha!"

Keil let his head flop back on the hard bench. TJ's leaps of logic were over the top. How he got from the fact Keil had a hard-on that could pound nails to making him Alpha was incredible.

"Enough. Can we let this drop for tonight? The problem will still be there in the morning."

TJ's laugh was long and loud, and finally Keil joined in.

"Okay, bad choice of words. Don't point it out."

Another howl rose from his brother, and Keil gave up. He grabbed the bucket of cool water and poured it over himself.

Evil thoughts intruded. He raised the other bucket. "Want a rinse?"

When TJ nodded, Keil grinned then poured the contents of the half-snow-filled bucket over his brother's head.

The icy-cold water streamed down as TJ's scream echoed in the small space.

Now Keil was ready for bed.

3

*K*eil rolled over for the millionth time.

This was impossible.

He'd slept in a cave surrounded by soaking wet, stinking pack members when they'd gotten caught in a storm. He'd slept in a single hotel room with seven buddies on a road trip, all of them snoring loud enough to shake the walls. Both times he'd gotten more sleep than tonight.

All because of the small female body at the end of the platform.

He gave up pretending and sat up to admire her better. The moonlight pouring in the window showed parts of her and his night vision filled in the rest of the details. She was curled into a half-circle, one leg pulled up, her head resting on a pillow made from her extra clothes. She wasn't in the sleeping bag, but under it, her body lying on a small soft blanket.

It was warm enough in the cabin she'd shrugged off most of her coverings and his gaze slipped over her. He wished he could touch her with his hands. Her skin tone was paler than his, her brown hair escaping from the ponytail she'd made before crawling into bed. Keil stared, memorizing the curve of her cheek, the dimple just visible at the edge of her mouth. Her eyes closed in sleep had the longest lashes he'd ever seen.

He licked his lips. Looking at her made his mouth water. He was tempted to slide over and take her in his arms, nestle her against his body and—

Shit. He was hard again.

How could she not know about belonging to a pack? As a full-blood wolf, she would have had the ability to shift from human form to wolf starting around adolescence. While the werewolf genes were dormant in most half-breeds, full-blood wolves almost always had their genes triggered while still babies.

Robyn being deaf was unusual, but not a huge issue. He could learn to sign, if that's what it took. When she was in wolf form, they'd have no problem communicating since wolf speak was ninety percent sign language. As mates, they should be able to speak into each other's minds anyway.

And if he was going to challenge for Alpha, there was an even greater chance he'd be able to hear her thoughts. One of the perks of heading a pack was a strong mental link to every member. Add that to the mate bond, and they'd be fine.

His mind slipped to pack problems even as his gaze continued to caress her. The current Alpha and Beta were getting too old to be proper leaders. The Granite pack was large and more transient than most with the constant influx of newcomers from the Lower 48.

Every time a wolf got the itch to connect with their inner self, they seemed to make their way north, thinking that the wilds of Alaska would help them *find themselves*. All they found was life required hard work, no matter where you lived. There was no easy ride anywhere, and perhaps even less here Up North.

Keil had begun to worry as more of their traditions fell away. It wasn't that he didn't like progress, but some things were tradition because it was good for the pack. Newcomers brought baggage with them, and a lot of what they were demanding the pack do to keep them comfortable went against everything the Granite pack stood for.

It was time for change. When the old leaders announced they would step aside and let someone younger take over, Keil knew it was his chance. He'd have to slow down on his guiding business, but having a strong pack would be worth it.

But he wasn't the only wolf with the potential to win the challenge. While another of the newcomers was his equal in strength, Jack's vision for the future of the pack traveled even further down the road to hell than the one they were currently on.

Keil groaned and rolled to his back. Finding his mate right now was going to make things difficult, to say the least. But was he sad he'd found her? Hell, no. Some wolves went their whole lives without discovering their mate. So he had a few issues to resolve?

Before next weekend. No rush.

A soft noise made him turn. Robyn was awake. She'd pushed up on one elbow, rubbing her hand over the side of her face and ear as if in pain. He scrambled closer, cautious not to frighten her—making sure she saw him approach.

He mouthed the words to avoid waking TJ. "Are you okay?"

Tears welled up in her eyes as she shook her head. With little effort he lifted her, pulling her into his arms. He ended up rubbing his hand over the side of her head while he rocked her gently back and forth. She was tense at first, but slowly relaxed, and his heart leapt.

Keil wasn't sure what was going on, but she felt too marvelous pressed up against him to think it through. His fingers continued to smooth over her hair and cheek, the feel of her against him wonderful and right. Her skin was soft under his fingers, the warmth of her torso wrapping around him like a blanket.

And when Robyn turned her head in his hand and caressed her cheek against his palm, he thought his heart would burst. He couldn't resist. Still cupping her face, he lowered his lips toward hers, brushing gently with a closed mouth, just to feel the friction of them coming together.

It was like a shock of electricity raced through her. Robyn had woken to the painful buzzing in her ear that had been a sporadic occurrence over the years. It only seemed to happen when she camped with strangers, and she'd learned to deal with it by rubbing, hard, on the soft spot below her ear. But today at Keil's gentle touch, the pain receded, and a wonderful warmth built throughout her body she'd never before experienced.

As his lips touched hers something clicked within her, and all she could think about was feeling him everywhere.

Oh, Lordy, she wanted to be naked with him, and that was really, really not her.

She'd reached twenty-six years old with limited sexual experience. Whether it was because her brother was overprotective, or because her deafness had scared away potential dates, she'd never worried about it too much. It wasn't as if she were totally ignorant—romance novels offered a great education, and she knew how to climax, but she'd never had any desire to try much of anything with anyone.

Her friends said she was saving herself for the "right man".

Her parents had told her when it was time, she'd know.

After all these years she'd figured that the Timex took a licking somewhere along the line and busted, because no one had really turned her crank.

Until now.

This stranger made her mouth water, and she hadn't had a real taste of him yet. She opened her lips a crack, to see what he'd do, and his eager tongue slipped in to trace the edge of her teeth.

Damn, he tasted good.

A sudden rush of scent filled her head and made it spin. Tingles raced down her body before landing between her legs. She reached out a hand to see if something was pushing on her crotch, but nothing was there except the internal pressure that made her want to squirm.

Keil's hand slipped to the back of her neck, drawing her closer and shifting her to a different angle as he continued to kiss her. She pressed into him, enjoying the sensations flowing through her.

Yet even as she kissed back she wondered what she was doing. Why she wasn't pulling her knife on him and getting him to back off?

He lifted her to lie on top of him as his tongue worked its magic. His heart pounded under her hands. The long, hard length of his body warm against her torso and limbs.

And she realized the long, hard length of something else nestled between her legs.

Oh. My. Word.

She pushed up with her hands on his hard chest to stare into dark brown eyes, uncertain what to do. She felt safe, even if this had to be the most insane thing she'd done in her life.

"Are you feeling better?" Keil mouthed as he traced a finger over the ear she'd been clutching moments earlier.

Robyn nodded.

"Let's get some more sleep. We'll talk this through in the morning, okay?"

She nodded again, leaning in to give him one more gentle kiss before crawling off his body to rearrange her sleeping space. Any concern over her strange reaction to him was washed away by the quick relief of her earache.

She'd just straightened the bottom blanket when a soft touch on her arm made her pause.

Keil's eyes were bewitching as he stared at her, before speaking. "Please, can I hold you?"

Robyn swallowed hard. Oh man, did she want him to hold her. She nodded before ducking her chin down to avoid his eyes.

He shifted his mattress closer, pulling her sleeping bag under them before wrapping an arm around her waist and drawing her back against his warm, solid body. He pulled his sleeping bag over the two of them, nestled her head on his arm, and wrapped his legs around hers, pinning her in place.

It was the most incredible feeling, safe and secure.

This was *insane*. She didn't know this man from Adam, and here she was, wrapped up like a jellyroll with him.

His fingers slipped along her arm to link with hers as he rested their joined hands against her belly.

Yup, totally insane.

She closed her eyes and fell asleep.

⁓

CLATTERING pots and pans woke Keil in the morning, and he groaned.

There were times that being deaf would be a blessing. Or at least make him stop wanting to kill his brother.

Wrapped up in Robyn's warmth, he wasn't ready to get out of bed yet.

They had shifted while asleep. He was flat on his back with her head resting on his chest. Her hands clutched him tightly while one of her legs had slipped over his belly, the inside of her thigh pressing his morning hard-on.

It was heaven and hell to feel the weight of her against him.

"So, I take it you've had an interesting night. It's also obvious I sleep like a log." TJ's grinning face peered down at them, his gaze tracing over Robyn as she clung to Keil's body. "Want me to make coffee, or do you want me to go ski for a few hours?"

"Stop leering at her. Nothing happened. Yes, make coffee and stop being such a shit." Keil tried to speak softly but she woke, reacting to the movement of his chest. "TJ, go get breakfast. I don't want her to be embarrassed."

"What's to be embarrassed about? She's your mate. You could do the horizontal bop in front of the pack, and no one would be embarrassed. Except Keith. He'd be embarrassed because he thinks he's got the biggest dick in the pack, and if you..."

TJ's voice faded as he dug into their food supplies for the coffee.

Keil sent up a prayer that Robyn wouldn't freak when she found herself in his arms. He didn't want to move backward in their relationship. He sensed today was going to be a big day. A day of big revelations. A day of—

"Ahhh."

He slammed his mouth shut as he grabbed her wrist. She'd slipped her leg off his cock when she woke, which was sad, but understandable. But she'd followed it by running her fingers over the hard length of him, and finished by cupping his balls.

"You okay, bro?" TJ wandered back with a worried expression on his face.

"Just fine. Um, leg cramp. Get the coffee."

"Yes, master. Right away, master."

Keil glanced down at Robyn who smiled back, a mischievous glint in her eyes he hadn't noticed the day before.

She mouthed the words, "leg cramp," and squeezed. Her face was flushed, but she was still smiling, and when she leaned up to kiss him, he thought he must have died and gone to heaven.

Whatever was happening, please don't let it stop.

Unfortunately, after brushing her lips over his she pushed herself upright, trailing her fingers over his torso in a maddening way before slipping from under the sleeping bag to go dress in her corner.

As he forced himself to ignore her, Keil watched TJ get out three cups and put on a big pan of ham steaks.

A clothed Robyn came back into his line of vision, and his brother stopped her.

"Good morning. Hey, how do you say that in sign language?"

She paused. She flipped him a thumbs up, and placing her left hand by her right elbow, she lifted her right hand in an arc.

TJ copied her. "Oh, cool, like the sun rising. Hey, Keil, look."

TJ signed good morning to him.

A chuckle from her made them both turn and regard her with amazement.

"You can laugh?" TJ asked.

Her smile fell away, and Keil swore inside.

She wrote a fast note then disappeared out the door.

He checked to make sure she was just headed for the outhouse before reading the message.

I'm deaf, not mute. Lost hearing as a child. Virus. I have an ugly voice. Two sugars, please.

TJ gave a soft whistle. "Man, oh man, is she going to be a handful. I'm glad she's your mate and not mine. Did you two fuck—?"

Keil hit him.

Not hard enough to do permanent damage, but hard enough to make TJ's eyes register the shock of it.

After picking himself up off the floor, his brother carefully exposed his neck, doing all the right things considering their positions in the Pack hierarchy.

"You will use that brain of yours to remember to be polite when you speak to and of my mate. Understood?" Keil drawled the words as he poured the coffee and prepared Robyn's cup. "Even though it's none of your damn business, if you were thinking straight you'd already know the answer. Use your bloody nose. No, we haven't mated yet. Yet for some insane reason, she let me kiss her and hold her, and while I'm pleased to report that yes, she's officially my mate, I have no idea why she doesn't seem to know a thing about wolves."

He dropped heavily into a chair by the table.

"So weird." TJ joined him, his moment of submissive posturing done.

"I don't want you making any stupid remarks until we figure this out. Got it?"

TJ shrugged. "I'll behave. I figure it might be kinda freaky to be told something like 'Hey, why didn't you know you're a werewolf and, oh, by the way, you're my mate. Oh, and there's going to be a challenge to the death next weekend for the leadership of our pack and I'm one of the headliners for the match.' Freaky, but...I think telling it all upfront might be the easiest way." He turned back and flipped the ham. "There's nowhere for her to run while we're here. Gives you time to work it out."

For the second time in as many days, the door behind them slammed open and Robyn charged in, her face red and her eyes blazing.

She glared back forth between the two of them, her nostrils flaring slightly.

For not knowing she was a wolf, she had the evil-eye thing down pretty good, Keil thought as a shiver ran down his spine. TJ struggled to keep his feet.

She surprised him by speaking. Her voice was gravelly and harsh, but very powerful. Keil had heard a few Alphas over the years, and she ranked up there with the best of them.

"Who is my mate?"

Like a flash, TJ pointed to Keil before swearing and stomping his feet like a disappointed child. "Oh, *crap*, has she got my number. I hope she doesn't tell me to go jump off a bridge or something because I'd—"

Robyn stormed up and grabbed the pad of paper.

Keil read over her shoulder as she wrote.

If you don't want to be overheard don't talk where a lip reader can see you.

Werewolf?

Mate.

Challenge. To the death.

What the HELL are you talking about?

She pulled away from the table, pausing to add, *Where is my coffee? And it had better be strong.*

4

*I*t took three hours, two pads of paper and fourteen fried ham-and-egg sandwiches.

Keil thought that on the whole it went pretty well, especially since he'd managed to not skin TJ alive during the interrogation.

Robyn stood stiff and angry at first, looking ready to throw her coffee cup if they made one wrong move.

"Come, sit down and we'll explain everything." He pulled back a chair for her, and she sat warily, shifting to keep both of them in her sight.

"Sorry, bro, guess my mouth got us both in trouble this time." TJ lightly touched Keil's arm in apology.

A sudden rumble of the floorboards made them both swing to look at her as she stomped her feet and glared evilly.

She pointed to the chairs and wrote rapidly, breaking the pencil lead as she underlined her final word.

I will talk this out with you. Sit down and don't you dare speak again when I can't see you. Ass.

Keil held out a reassuring hand and sat, motioning for

TJ to join them. "I understand. We'll answer your questions. What do you want to know?"

Robyn found another pencil and opened to a new page. *Don't think because I went a little crazy last night and let you touch me you can jerk me around this morning. You're insane, right? Escaped from some home?*

"No, it's true. We're able to turn into wolves."

Prove it. She leaned back in her chair and stared at them mockingly.

The two men exchanged glances.

What? You need a full moon?

Both men dropped their heads into their hands for a moment. Bloody fairy tales. Finally Keil looked up to see her very confused expression.

"No. Mature wolves don't need a full moon. We also don't bite people to turn them into werewolves. You either have the genes, or you don't. Sorry, that's one of those tall tales that drives us crazy. We'll have to, umm, take off our clothes to change." Keil watched Robyn's face. A blush rose to colour her cheeks and her eyes brightened with the mischief he'd seen earlier in the morning.

Good, maybe this wouldn't take too much damage control.

She flipped the pad across the table. *A private strip show? Goodie. Even if you don't turn into anything, the morning isn't a complete write-off.*

Keil laughed and turned to TJ.

His brother knew immediately what Keil expected, but TJ offered a protest. "You should be the one to strip. She's gonna see you naked the most often."

Keil glared at his brother.

"What? You still having problems with that boner? Man, now I really think you should shift. It would serve you right for hauling me along on your retreat instead of letting me go hang out at Klondyke Kate's with the rest of the pack."

"TJ," he snarled.

"All right, don't get your fur in a knot. I'll shift, but you keep an eye on her. If she signs anything that looks like 'cute doggy' or 'sweet fluffy wuffy', I want to learn them to insult the boys at the next pack meeting."

Robyn raised a brow.

"Stop it with the Spock look, that seriously freaks me out. I keep expecting to see you grow pointy ears and hear you announce, 'But this is not logical.'" TJ continued rambling as he dropped his clothes to stand naked in the middle of the cabin.

He waggled his eyebrows at her, and she blushed harder.

"Get on with it before I apply the Vulcan death grip, little brother." Keil spoke through clenched teeth.

TJ shimmered, and there were two images overlapping each other, another shimmer and there was a large silver grey wolf sitting on its haunches in front of them.

Robyn tensed then rose from her chair, eyes wide with wonder. She stood for the longest time and simply stared, her breathing rapid, face flushed.

He was ready to take her arm to reassure her when she dropped to her knees and reached out in slow motion to brush the fur on TJ's head and neck.

After a few strokes of her hand, TJ rolled over to his back and tilted his neck up

A surge of pleasure raced through Keil's veins at the sight. His brother, while not always the sharpest knife in the drawer, was a physically strong wolf. TJ didn't give instant obeisance to just anyone. Another indicator that the woman kneeling by Keil's feet was going to be a powerful addition in his life.

TJ shifted back and Robyn was caught stroking her hand down his naked chest.

"Damn!" she shouted and shot away from TJ, backing into the door.

"Oops, sorry. You were tickling me something fierce. Boy, am I glad you didn't say 'shit' or some other swear word like that. With how strong your voice is, I'd have been in a hell of a mess," TJ muttered quietly as he pulled on his clothes.

She closed her eyes for a moment and drew a shaky breath. Hell, could TJ do anything without screwing it up?

Keil refilled her coffee cup and waited for her to open her eyes before patting the seat next to him to get her to settle in close.

He wanted to pat his lap and have her crawl into it like last night. Actually, he wanted to strip her down and crawl into her, but that was going to take a little more time and patience on his part.

He hated being patient.

Her head was spinning, her heart beat a million times a minute and somewhere along the line she must have fallen down a rabbit hole.

Tad was never going to believe this. She was having trouble believing it, and she'd seen TJ change. She'd touched his wolf form. It wasn't an illusion.

Unless there'd been something in her coffee. She gave it a cautious sniff. Smelt like normal Midnight Sun brew. She glanced up to see Keil watching her, his gorgeous eyes dark and dangerous. A shiver raced down her spine and heat flared in her belly.

Damn, he was potent.

She grabbed the notepad and sat for a bit thinking what to write. She twisted her face up, tapped the pencil a few times while biting her lip. Finally she went for honest.

Well. I'll admit it. That was pretty cool.

Keil smiled, and she melted some more. Between his smile and the expression in his eyes, moisture was pooling in her mouth. And farther south.

She took a quick sip of her coffee and dragged her eyes away from his.

So what makes you think I'm a wolf? I've never turned into anything.

"You smell like wolf." TJ leaned forward in his chair and sniffed in her direction. "Yup. I can't explain it better than that. I can't have you sniff a human and then sniff a wolf 'cause, we're all wolves here. But when we go back to civilization, we can show you. Well, even there it's tough to explain to someone that you need to sniff them, but don't want to say why. Trust us. You're a wolf."

Keil nodded in agreement, and Robyn shifted in her chair to stare out the window. A tidal wave of emotions swept over her. The ability to turn into a wolf. Who wouldn't want to be able to do that? It was the stuff of fairy tales and escape literature everywhere.

It also called to something deep inside her that had felt cooped up and trapped for many years. While she enjoyed her job at the bakery, and she loved her brother, she was never completely happy unless she was somewhere out in nature—skiing or hiking or canoeing.

Maybe this was the reason.

She pushed the notepad at TJ. *How come I've never turned furry?*

TJ wrinkled his nose and considered for a minute. "Keil? Ideas?"

Keil stroked her arm absentmindedly as he considered, and she bit back a moan. Oh man, that felt good. Her skin itched to be touched, and as much as she needed to find answers, she needed to jump Keil more. The attraction that had begun last night, causing her to lose all sense and sleep in the man's arms, seemed to be growing.

Concentrate. She needed to concentrate on the cool idea that she might actually be able to turn into a wolf.

"Okay, a little background info," Keil said. "Full-blood wolves like us are born with the genes to be able to shift, but they're turned off in newborns until triggered. Kind of like they're dormant. For some reason your genes must have never been switched on."

A trigger?

Keil nodded. "Yeah. It's a hormone, and newborns get it from their mom's milk."

Robyn's stomach fell. It more than fell, it leapt off the edge of Mount Logan and plummeted into the depths of the nearest crevasse.

The possibility that she was a magical being had excited her. Seeing TJ change had woken something inside her, full of joy and freedom, and a deep happiness she'd been missing all her life.

Now it was slipping out of her reach and there was nothing she could do to stop it.

She pushed away from the table and grabbed her coat. Keil rose to his feet, but she ignored his outstretched hand, fighting back the tears as she rushed outside.

Damn, it wasn't fair.

She managed to get her coat done up before the tears fell. She stood gazing over the lake, arms wrapped tightly around her torso as her eyes welled up and overflowed. The bright sunshine around her did nothing to lighten the spot of darkness she felt at the loss of something she'd wanted. Something she hadn't realized she'd wanted so much.

Even crying like a baby, Robyn felt him approach. Gentle arms slipped around her torso and pulled her back against his body, supporting her. Holding her loosely enough she could escape if she wanted, but close enough to let her feel his concern.

Another sob escaped before she could stop it, and Keil turned her, gathering her up as if she was a child.

She wrapped her arms around his neck, buried her face in his coat and let the misery release.

Her heart hurt.

Slowly, feeling his strength, feeling the comfort he offered, the pain eased. He ran a hand over her hair, and she remembered him touching her like that last night. He must think she was some kind of emotional yo-yo, running hot then cold. She took a deep breath and sniffed hard, pulling away from his embrace.

He cupped her face, wiping away a tear with his thumb. "I'm not sure what's wrong, but I think I've guessed a bit. Did something happen to your mom when you were born?"

Robyn nodded. She patted her pockets searching for tissue. He handed her a clean hankie. It took a minute to get herself back together. Keil politely ignored her runny nose and wet face until she felt presentable.

She flicked glances up at him as he stood waiting. He gazed over the lake, his strong body like a pillar of granite. What was it about this man that fascinated her so?

He turned to see if she was ready, holding out a hand to

her. She grasped his warm fingers, enjoying the tingling sensation that raced up her arm as he wrapped his fingers around hers and led her back into the cabin.

Inside Keil refused to talk. Instead he made her up a plate of food and sat beside her while he ate his own meal.

The lump in her throat settled, aided by the fact that sitting in close proximity to Keil made her mouth water, and she had to swallow twice as often as usual.

TJ spoke while he ate, which made for confusing moments as Robyn misread most of what he said. She was good at reading lips—but not *that* good. He was telling her all about their pack and how they spent time together in human form as well as in wolf. At one point she was sure that he said something about mooning people down main-street Haines, but that had to have been the extra large piece of sandwich he'd shoved in his mouth.

Breakfast finished, Robyn had to admit she felt better. Having an emotional breakdown on an empty stomach was too much.

Keil grabbed her dishes and kissed her softly on the cheek. "We'll wash up, you write. Tell me what's got you worried."

His dark eyes stayed on her until she nodded, then he turned away and got to work. He and TJ goofed off with the dishtowels and soap bubbles while they cleaned up the dishes and tidied the sleeping bags. She sipped at her coffee as she watched, the love between the brothers clear.

She forced herself to pull the pad closer and write. When she finished, she found Keil staring at her from where he sat waiting on the edge of the sleeping platform. His gaze ran over her body, and he wasn't trying to hide the look of desire on his face. Their eyes met, and the shock of connection thrilled through her.

The wolf thing. It had to be something to do with animal attraction that was making her want to roll all over the floor with the man. Preferably naked.

She licked her lips involuntarily, and the answering flash in his eyes heated her blood to near boiling.

Damn, it was time to stop with the coffee and break out the ice water.

Keil tapped the space next to him and held out a hand for the notepad. "Come here. Sit by me while I read."

She took a step toward him then paused, glancing toward TJ who was sprawled in a chair in front of the stove, making notes in the cabin's journal.

"He's going to let us talk this out alone," Keil informed her.

Robyn sat, highly aware of the feel of his thigh touching hers as he shifted his body to wrap an arm around her torso and snuggle her tightly to his side. If she looked up she could still see his lips move.

In fact his lips were close enough to kiss if she leaned forward a tiny bit.

She whipped her head back to safety, examining the notepad and the message she'd written.

My mother and father were hunting caribou along the Dempster Highway when there was an accident at their hunting camp. Someone's gun went off and the bullet killed my father instantly and wounded my mother, sending her into shock. The others at the camp managed to get her to the hospital at Dawson City where I arrived almost two months early. When my mother died right after my delivery, I was adopted. All I have from my parents is my boot knife.

I guess that's why I never got "triggered"? I can't turn into a wolf.

I wish I could. I bet it's amazing.

She glanced up to see if he'd finished reading.

He smiled tenderly. "It's going to be all right. I'll explain a couple things first to help you understand."

He ripped off the top sheet of the notepad to a clean page. She watched over his arm as he divided the page in three parts and drew a circle in each part. In the top circle he wrote *Full-blood*, in the bottom he wrote *Half-blood*. He left the middle one empty.

He adjusted position until they were both comfortable on the platform but he could face her better.

"Short biology lesson, Robyn. Full-blood werewolf, both Mom and Dad have the genes. Pass the dormant gene to baby. Baby triggered with hormones in milk, can turn to wolf around puberty." He lowered the notepad for a moment. "And if you think that teenage humans are moody, wait until you see an angst-ridden fifteen-year-old wolf. Very scary."

She snorted. He winked then continued.

"Half-blood, only one parent has wolf genes. They're still passed on to the baby, dormant, but for some reason even milk from a werewolf mom won't trigger them. The hormones have to come from something else." Robyn watched as Keil wrote *milk* across from the top circle. He paused before writing *sex* across from the bottom circle.

"Half-blood wolves can get triggered by having sex with a full-blood. The hormones released during unprotected sex work fast, and since wolves can't get STDs, it's both effective and safe. There's a little added complication for males because of something called 'FirstMate', but females don't have to worry about that." He stopped and Robyn swallowed hard.

Well. That was a bit of a surprise.

One circle left to fill in. She watched as he wrote her name in the empty space.

Oh shit. She knew where this was going.

She grabbed the pen and flipped over the page, crawling away from him on the platform to write. She might have the hots for the man. No way was he going to use a biology lesson to get into her pants.

You want to have sex with me?

The flash of hot desire in his eyes answered the question faster than his mouth could.

"Hang on, Robyn. There's one more thing I need to explain. And that's all I'm doing, explaining. You get to make any decisions you want based on what I tell you. Trust me."

She hesitated and then insistently shook the notepad at him. If he didn't 'fess up she was going to hit him.

"Hell, yes, I want to make love with you. But that's because you're my mate."

Her fingers were awkward as she scrambled to respond. *Convenient. Maybe I should ask TJ if he wants to fuck me, too.*

Keil burst with a roar that she felt down to her bones. "No one else is going to fuck you, especially not TJ!"

Out of the corner of her eye she saw TJ fly backward off his chair to land in a puddle on the floor, eyes wide as he turned his attention toward them.

"Holy crap, Keil, what are you telling her?" TJ must not have liked the answer because he cowered lower on the floor. "Well, hurry it up. Listening to one side of your conversation is scaring me to death."

Robyn considered for a moment then held up her hand to Keil. She snuck over to TJ and wrote *him* a note.

Even if they'd rehearsed this, she didn't think TJ was

fast enough to try and pull one over on her. He'd be forced to tell her the truth.

Keil says he's my mate. What does that mean, and how can I tell if it's true?

"Hey, bro, she's asking me about you."

Robyn stepped back toward the sleeping platform keeping her eyes firmly on TJ, which meant she missed Keil's response and only got TJs eyeroll and next words.

"Of course I won't touch her. But you still need to promise you won't hurt me."

Keil must have answered calmly enough to reassure TJ, who finally crawled off the ground. He wrinkled up his face and gazed upward, rubbing a finger over his lips as if trying to remember something. Shortly, he nodded to himself and turned to face both Robyn and Keil.

"Okey dokey. Mates are like getting married, only better for five reasons." He held up a hand and lifted a finger with each comment he made. "First, mates have similar interests and tastes. Second, the chemical attraction between mates makes it impossible to miss knowing they are 'the one'. Third, sex between mates is super-hot and stays that way for their entire lives. Fourth, mates are connected deeper than physically—there's a mental and emotional connection too. And finally, mates never, ever fool around on each other." TJ looked at Keil who stood with his mouth dropped open in amazement. "Pretty good, hey? Mark and I wrote that up for the pack chicks when they wanted to do a wolf version of a Cosmo 'Find Your Perfect Mate' quiz."

TJ grabbed Robyn by the hand and pulled her with him as he went to stand next to Keil. "How you can tell it's true is easy. Remember, bro, you said you wouldn't hurt me. Robyn, give me a kiss."

Keil stiffened up, and Robyn was a little shocked, as

well. If it were possible to be *more* shocked this particular morning.

"Just on the cheek! Check out my scent and how it makes you feel. Then kiss Keil. That'll explain better than words." He turned his face to the side, keeping a wary eye on his brother.

She bit her lip. She didn't need to do this "test" of TJ's. She knew what he was saying already. She knew she was sexually attracted to Keil. Completely and utterly attracted.

But doing the test meant she could kiss him again.

She leaned toward TJ and took a long breath in through her nose. Nothing but the smell of dish soap and the slightly earthy scent of a male missing his morning shower. She touched his cheek with her lips and felt like she did when she kissed Tad.

Connected, like family. No fireworks.

She shifted her weight and stared up into Keil's beautiful eyes. She started to take a deep breath but stopped quickly. His scent filled her. She could taste him, feel him slip down into her lungs and throughout her whole body. He smelt like the air of a starlit night, and dark-chocolate fondue and raw, passionate sex.

Unable to stop herself, she ignored his offered cheek and grasped him by the hair, pulling him down to her reach so she could clasp their mouths together.

As Keil reacted, their tongues tangling together, Robyn acknowledged that she'd never felt anything like the satisfaction she experienced at every contact with the big man in front of her.

Well, it seemed she was getting hitched.

5

"This doesn't mean we'll do anything until you're ready," Keil said when he finally managed to drag himself away from her. "We can take our time, and get to know each other first. Now that I've found you, I can wait."

Her bright eyes shone back at him.

TJ bumped up from behind.

"Umm, Keil, but what about—"

Keil swung his elbow back and connected with TJ's gut.

"Ugh." The air whooshed out of TJ, but he struggled on. "I'm just saying—"

Keil turned to face his brother, careful to hold Robyn close enough that she couldn't read his lips. "No, you're not saying another word about this. Understand?" It was a command, said in a tone that TJ couldn't ignore.

Robyn wasn't the only one with the Alpha voice.

TJ froze. He dropped his eyes. "Understood."

Keil pushed Robyn away a bit and winked at her. "It's been a tough morning, and I think we could use some exercise. Ski to the top of the pass for lunch?"

She nodded with enthusiasm and slipped away to change.

Keil wanted to give her some time alone to think about everything she'd learned, but his wolf refused to let her head out unprotected.

Split personalities were tough to deal with at the best of times, and right now, his wolf was pissed. It didn't see what the problem was and why there was no marking and mating happening.

Me too, bud, Keil thought.

He let his eyes trace over Robyn's hips as she tucked in her long-sleeved undershirt. In his mind he could already feel the weight of her body slipping over his shaft as he held onto those hips and helped her ride him. His aching cock pressed up against his ski pants and he had to adjust himself.

Again.

Yup, he was all for making the sacrifice to help her be able to shift to wolf.

Part of him wanted to send TJ back to civilization ahead of time, giving them some privacy. Only with the way TJ skied, he couldn't be left alone. The boy would probably get lost, or break a ski, or have some other disaster.

Damn. Trapped in the bush with his mate and an unwanted chaperone.

No, it was for the best. He needed to give Robyn time to adjust. Time to talk to her family, and be able to accept the changes that would take place if she triggered her wolf.

It wouldn't be fair either to make her full wolf and his mate if he died in the challenge on Sunday. It would be far better to wait until after the weekend when he'd have the proper time and energy to court her.

Even if it made every cell in his body scream in protest at the thought of waiting.

He watched as she removed three avalanche monitors from the shelf and set them to the same frequency, checking the blinking lights to be sure they worked.

"No way, Keil. Oh man, you know I hate wearing those things. Tell her I don't have to," TJ whined.

Robyn held out the devices to the men, her eyebrow rising at the sight of TJ pulling back and hiding his hands behind his back.

"I hate them."

Her shrug said she didn't care what he thought as she stepped up to him, slipped the strap over his neck and fastened the waist belt. She patted TJ's pouting cheek while she batted her eyes and gave him an evil grin.

"I feel like a dog with a collar."

Robyn snorted and turned to make sure Keil wore his monitor correctly.

"I do this for a living. You'll get no complaints from me." He adjusted the straps around her waist, unkinking a section of elastic to make it lie flat against her body.

His fingers traced along the straps stretching over her torso, and his heartbeat increased at the feel of her under his hands. He looked up and saw her watching him. She swallowed hard, and her tongue darted out to moisten her bottom lip.

"It'll feel better if it's even under your coat." He paused for a moment touching the tops of her hipbones. She was halfway into the embrace of his arms, and he wanted nothing more than to complete the move and pull her to him. To feel her pressed along his whole torso. To lower his mouth to hers and taste her.

She shifted as he leaned closer, temptation pulling him,

her eyes drawing him like a magnet. Closer and closer her mouth came to his as he reached around her body with his hands to caress her back.

A sudden sharp pain shot through his left buttock, shoving him hard into Robyn's body as they careened backward toward the table.

"What the—?" Keil roared as he grasped Robyn and swung her around to avoid crushing her.

Behind them TJ threw gear left and right as he dug through his pack. His ski poles were tucked under his arm, extended backward, and every move he made shot the pointed tips in their direction.

"You bloody fool!" Keil attempted to grab the moving poles, but they kept dancing out of reach. A sudden extra enthusiastic twist by TJ forced the poles hard toward them.

Keil pushed Robyn to the side as he shouted, "TJ, freeze!"

The solid *thunk* of the ski tip spearing into the wood table finally pulled TJ away from his rummaging to look closer at them.

Robyn and Keil stood side by side, the ski pole quivering as it jutted into the room from between their hips. TJ's innocent expression was beyond irritating.

"What?"

"TJ, you're a menace to everyone around you." Keil growled as he yanked the offending pole out and held it to his brother.

"How did that get there?"

Keil twisted toward Robyn and, placing a hand on her shoulder, made sure she could see his lips move.

"Is there an appropriate sign to tell my younger brother that he's a shithead, and if he doesn't watch it, I'll tie him to the outhouse with a short leash?"

Robyn made a show of turning to face TJ and shaking her arms. Then she slowly raised her hand and flipped TJ her middle finger.

"Yeah," Keil said, "I thought that should about cover it."

~

THEY SKIED single file down to the lake, Robyn following Keil as he broke trail. He insisted on going first and she fought back a laugh. He was very much like her brother, Tad, refusing to let anyone work harder than him.

Still, it gave her time to let her mind wander as she simply followed the ridges he left in the snow. While everything she'd been told this morning seemed to be impossible, the proof of TJ's change into his wolf form made it clear that this wasn't some practical joke they were trying to pull.

There was also the matter of her instant attraction to the large male striding in front of her. Robyn lifted her gaze to watch him ski, efficient as he worked to make tracks in the foot of soft snow that lay on the surface of the frozen lake. Something about him fascinated her.

Like a deer in the headlights of a fast-approaching truck, she was waiting for the impact to knock her silly.

The pheromones between the two of them were cooking hot. Before the little ski-pole incident, she thought she was going to end up as a snack. Heck, she'd wanted to be nibbled on. Tingles ran all over her body even thinking about Keil and his touch.

The way she'd been wrapped up around him when she woke this morning, the reaction of his body to her touch. The strange way he was able to comfort her in the middle of the night. The usual repercussions from an earache would have her moving slowly for the whole day, with a nagging headache to boot. One touch of his hand, a little cuddle, and the pain had drained away.

They were like a stick of dynamite and a Bic lighter. Too much more time together and something was going to blow.

She sighed as she wished for the hundredth time that Tad were here to bounce ideas off of.

Her brother. Was he a wolf too? He'd never said anything. If this was news to him, was he going to be surprised.

Of course if he already knew she might have to kill him.

She could already hear him complain about her acting irresponsibly and doing this trip alone. Tad always said she was going to end up meeting some strange wackos in the backcountry.

He probably hadn't thought she'd meet someone who wanted to turn her into a werewolf.

As they approached the bottom of the pass, Keil stopped and dropped his daypack. Robyn joined him and the two spent a moment enjoying the view, the sunshine on the snow, the mountains rising boldly around them.

Keil nudged her arm, passing his water bottle after taking a long drink. He licked a drop of water left on his lip, and a warm buzz shot through her. There was something erotic about sharing a water bottle that she'd never noticed before in any previous backcountry trip.

She took a sip, very aware of Keil's eyes watching her mouth, watching her throat move as she swallowed.

She lowered the bottle slowly and smiled at him. This courting business was going to be fun.

"I'll head uphill. Wait for TJ and make sure he takes a drink. He's known for getting dehydrated. Okay?" He brushed his fingers over her lips in a gentle caress before turning away.

Robyn stared as Keil traveled smoothly up the hill on an angle, his powerful body setting the difficult trail with seeming ease.

Wow. Mates with Mr. Studmuffin. How did she get so lucky?

Only there was trouble in paradise. Something had happened this morning right before they set out. TJ was upset, and he'd been fine until Keil had cut him off.

Time to find out why.

It took a few minutes for TJ to catch up. She handed him the water bottle, holding it a second longer than necessary to force him to take a close look at her. When she was sure that he was watching, she motioned toward Keil with her head. She tapped her fingers together like they were lips speaking.

TJ bit his lip. "Ah, man, this is unfair. Keil told me to stay quiet. You gotta understand, as a human, he's my brother and I feel loyalty to him. He's also the most powerful wolf I know, and it actually hurts to think about disobeying him."

Robyn pointed to Keil and herself followed by linking her fingers together.

"Yeah, I know you guys are gonna be joined as mates. That means you're strong enough that it hurts to think about disobeying you too." He tilted his head to the side and with a pained expression asked, "I don't suppose I can talk you into letting me off the hook?"

Robyn felt guilty for pushing him, but there was something here that she needed to know.

She spoke out loud. Soft but clear.

"Tell me."

"Arghhhhh! Damn. Fine, I'll spill. He didn't tell you the whole truth about mates. It's not something you can put off that easy. He's trying to give you time to adjust to the whole idea of being a wolf and all that. He's being noble." TJ stared up the hillside where his brother was making the first switchback. "Keil is going to challenge for the leadership of our pack on Sunday. He's way stronger than the other guy, and I know Keil can win.

"Only the challenge is in both human and wolf form, and it can get a little messy, especially if either challenger's wolf isn't under control.

"The longer you two wait to finish mating, the more distracted his wolf is going to get. I'm not trying to get you into bed with Keil... Well, yeah, I am. The sooner, the better. Because if you don't get marked and mated before the weekend, His wolf is going to be so agitated that I'm afraid for the outcome of the challenge."

TJ swung his gaze back to meet hers. "I'm afraid for you too, because it could be dangerous to be around the pack. Since you and Keil kissed and snuggled last night, your wolf has started to rise to the surface, and you're giving off sex pheromones like crazy. All of the unmated males are going to be real interested. I don't think Keil's aware of it because he's attracted to you already. I feel it, but I know you're his, and I'm making myself ignore it."

She nodded her understanding and reached to brush TJ's cheek in thanks with a quick touch. His eyes closed for a second, then he coughed.

"Um, Robyn? You need to know, wolves are into touchy-feely stuff, and as much as I like you to pet me, you'd better not do that again until after you and Keil get hitched. 'Cause right now I don't think he could stand to scent you on anyone, and I'm kinda fond of my balls staying attached to my body."

He handed back the water bottle and motioned for her to take the lead up the hill.

They climbed, using the long shallow switchbacks Keil had set to make the ascent easier. Robyn glanced over her shoulder to see TJ following behind, slow and steady, his skis skittering off to the side every few steps. He was terribly uncoordinated on two feet.

By the time they reached the top of the pass, she was sweating nicely and feeling a warm glow of satisfaction from the exertion. Keil had pulled out a small cook stove and fired it up to heat water for a drink.

"You're a good skier, Robyn. Kept the pace nicely." Keil's compliment warmed her as she sat facing him, able to look over the mountains that ranged downward to the Pacific Ocean and still see his face. She breathed a relaxed sigh as she let her gaze wander over the sunlit peaks.

A squeeze on her knee brought her attention back to Keil.

"You hungry?"

She nodded and pulled her pack closer to dig out the food she'd brought. She passed him a couple of her homemade granola bars and watched as pleasure bloomed on his face as he bit into them.

"These are delicious. Did you buy them in Whitehorse?"

She shook her head *no, then* nodded *yes* while pointing to herself.

"You didn't buy them, but you got them. Did you make them?"

She nodded.

The admiration in his eyes increased. "Hmmmm. She

cooks, too." He leaned forward slowly and planted a gentle kiss on her lips. They stared at each other for a minute, desire rising between them like a tangible cloud before the boiling water brought Keil back to earth.

"You guys are too fast." TJ's red face as he dropped beside Keil made Robyn laugh. "Oh sure, laugh it up at the slowpoke. I'll have you know that once you can shift to wolf, I'll be able to beat your butt in a race anytime. Right, Keil?"

Keil handed her a cup of hot, sweet tea. "Other than suggesting you not even think about Robyn's butt ever again, I will agree that you are very fast as a wolf. Robyn, I know this has been an information overload with everything we've thrown at you—"

She waved her hand to cut him off. She deliberately turned her back on him and pointed over the mountains, over the whole panorama until she faced them.

TJ got the message. "She's right. Shut up for a minute and enjoy the view."

"I know, but—"

"But nothing. It's too hard to talk right now. Relax. Or don't you know how? You need to lighten up a little, bro. It's not all pack politics, life-and-death situations, Captain Kirk, I mean Keil, to the rescue."

When TJ finished speaking, Robyn glanced at Keil and nodded. She held her hand to him and he rose to join her. She pulled off her glove to trace her fingers down his cheek before twisting around and settling her back against him as she admired the view.

He was very serious, she realized. He couldn't be much older than she was, and he was planning on taking on the leadership of a large group of, well, if she guessed right, rather headstrong individuals.

She could help him learn to relax. She stifled a giggle.

His strong arms supported her, coming around her torso and pulling her tight to his rock-solid frame. Too bad winter clothing made everything extra bulky, but she could still appreciate the feel of his firm body.

She turned and slipped her hands behind his neck. As their lips brushed together, she tightened her hold and lifted her feet off the ground to let her full body weight drag at him.

The surprise move worked, and they fell to the snow. Robyn tried to slip away as they hit the ground, but he held her, rolling to end up lying on top and pinning her in place.

"That was sneaky." Keil stared at her, shifting his hips to let her know she was trapped. "I think you should pay a forfeit for that little trick." He lowered his head and nuzzled against her neck, and she felt him taking deep breaths. His tongue shot along her bare skin, and she shivered as a wave of desire scurried through her body, over her breasts and settled in her core like a ticking time bomb.

Man, oh man, this guy was potent.

With a final kiss to her neck, he rose from her body and pulled her to her feet.

"It's getting late, and if we want to get back to the cabin in daylight, we'd better ski. Stay away from the right side on the descent, the snow seems unstable." Robyn nodded, swallowing hard from the extra moisture in her mouth. Keil traced a finger over her lips and winked at her. "I'll claim my forfeit back at the cabin."

The three of them packed up their things, and this time Robyn led the way, skiing down the side of the mountain using telemark turns. She stopped a quarter of the way down and waited for the others to catch up. Keil stopped beside her, TJ farther to the side.

"Nice turns." Keil said. "Let me go first, I want to watch

you from below this time." He set off, making the lunging motions that cause cross-country skis to turn in the deep snow of the mountainside.

She admired his skill as well. The people that she and Tad skied with in the mountains were all experts, and Keil would fit in just fine.

She caught up with him, and they both turned to watch TJ do his descent.

His bright red jacket looked good, and that was the most positive thing she could say about his technique. TJ didn't ski, he threw his legs about in a mad scramble like he was wearing rollerblades. Ski poles rotated in the air, snow flew everywhere. Robyn bit her lip to keep from laughing.

Then her breath caught in her throat. The snow slab dropped, and a large crack appeared on the hillside above where TJ headed, too far into the danger zone and completely out of control.

She stared in horror as the side of the mountain behind TJ slid away in an avalanche, pulling his windmilling figure down the slope to the right of them. The ground underfoot shook for a moment, but the snow pack where they stood was solid enough.

Frantically she looked back and forth over the settling powder and clouds of fine snow to try to see any sign of TJ.

Nothing but the disturbed surface of the mountainside greeted their eyes.

6

His stomach dropped as the avalanche raced past them. By the time the rumble faded, Keil had his transmitter out and switched to "seek" mode. They didn't have much time to uncover TJ, but they did have longer than finding a human.

As long as TJ was conscious.

Keil turned to Robyn. She already had her transmitter in her hand. She was pale, and her eyes seemed large enough to overwhelm her face, but she was going through each step methodically. Carefully.

He grabbed her face in his hands, making sure she watched him.

"You know how to use your monitor?"

She nodded.

"Since you can't hear me if I shout, I want you to look at me every five paces, to be sure you're aware of any warning I give. Understand?"

Robyn nodded again even as she shuffled away from him. She pointed up the mountain.

"Yes, you go up. If I signal 'clear' like this"—Keil slapped his fists together and pointed away with one hand—"I expect you to ski away as fast as you can. Understand?"

Her face grew grim and tight.

"I mean it. If you get caught in another avalanche, I won't be able to save you both. Remember, TJ's a werewolf. He's stronger than a human. He's going to be all right. Let's go."

The two of them skied quickly to the edge of the avalanche field and began a back-and-forth search motion to triangulate TJ's position. Keil moved cautiously, his attention split between rescuing TJ and the need to keep Robyn safe.

Letting his mate move away from him into the potential danger of another slide physically hurt.

His senses were on high alert. The sun reflecting off the snow seemed blindingly bright. The squeak of their skis on the rough snow surface became reassuring in its consistency. A few steps, a pause to check the monitor, a glance around the mountain. A flick of the eyes to reassure himself she was safe, then repeat the series.

The blinking light on his receiver grew stronger, and he turned to follow its direction.

The next time she looked his way, he raised an arm and pointed.

Robyn double-checked her monitor and raised her arm, pointing downhill in a path that bisected across his angle.

They were narrowing the gap.

It was painfully slow work when every nerve in his body screamed for them to hurry before TJ's air ran out. Keil took a moment to call out. "TJ!" He yelled in the direction he hoped they'd find TJ, but there was no response.

A trickle of sound reached his ears.

A low rumble in the distance.

He lifted his gaze to examine the mountains around them, fearful of what he'd see.

The peak to their left released a cornice of snow, the slide shifting a cloud of powder into the air. Quickly, he estimated the angle of the slide, whether it would reach them, set off another slide on top of them.

The slope of the mountain curved away, and he breathed a sigh of relief as the loose snow slipped behind a distant ridge out of sight and out of range of danger.

He looked up to see Robyn watching intently for his signal. Escape or continue?

He pointed forward. She nodded, trusting his judgment as she resumed her sweeping movements.

Her harsh shout a few moments later made his heart pound. He looked up to see her turning her ski pole into a depth probe. She pushed it through the snow to search for an air pocket or a buried body. He struggled up to her level, whipped off his shovel and prepared to dig.

"TJ, can you hear us?" Keil roared.

A welcomed howl rose to his ears.

He threw up a prayer of thanks as he shoveled, Robyn working at his side. They dug into the hillside from the bottom to take advantage of the slope, trusting there would be less digging at that level.

It seemed an eternity before he held out a hand in warning.

"I don't want to strike him. Let me dig, you watch for additional slides."

Keil increased his speed, hearing TJ's howl grow clearer.

"Stay back from the shovel if you've got the room," he shouted as he swung at a furious pace. It was only a few more shovelfuls before he broke into the human-sized air pocket that contained the smaller wolf-sized body that was TJ.

His brother scrambled out of the hole and, in his wolf body, circled around their legs in thanks.

~

TJ SAT in front of the fire in the cabin sipping a steaming cup of hot chocolate. He'd run beside them all the way to the cabin as a wolf, his gear buried somewhere back on the hill.

"I still don't get it. What part of 'stay away from the right, the snow is unstable' did you not understand?" Keil complained, dropping an extra blanket around TJ's shoulders.

"Enough, I'm sorry. I got my lefts and rights mixed up. No harm done since Robyn made me put on the tracer. You found me, I'm fine."

"TJ, that's the third set of skis you've lost this year!"

The sound of logs crashing to the floor made both of them look up at her stunned expression. She lifted a trembling hand to show three raised fingers, a questioning expression on her face.

"Yeah," Keil said, "this is the third time Mr. Disaster has been in action this winter. His record is six times in a single season. I'm thinking of having a tracer permanently implanted—"

"Umm, Keil, why is she glaring at me like that?"

Keil glanced up. He could have sworn he saw steam pouring out of her ears just before she leapt across the room, grabbed TJ by the throat and shook him.

Hard.

"Whoa, there." Reaching around her, he gently grasped her forearms and loosened them from TJ's neck. Muttering soothing words even though he knew she couldn't hear, he settled her under his chin as her body continued to shake. "My guess is she's a little shocked we had to rescue you in the first place, TJ, and learning this is a typical experience in the bush with you might be more than she needed on top of everything else today."

TJ had the grace to look embarrassed. He shuffled over and knelt low so he could peer up at her where she hid in Keil's arms. "I'm sorry I scared you. I don't think sometimes. I won't do it again."

"Ha!" Keil snorted. "Don't make promises you can't keep, little brother. The sauna should be hot by now. Go get warmed up all the way. Robyn and I need to talk."

TJ shot another concerned glance at her before gathering his clothes and heading out the door.

Keil settled down on the chair by the fire, still holding Robyn as they sat quietly together. Having her in his arms felt wonderful. She was small enough to treasure, yet strong enough to react in a quick and fearless manner when faced with the emergency on the mountainside.

She was going to be a fabulous mate for him.

She smelt wonderful too. He took in a deep breath and fought down the urge to throw her on the sleeping platform and rip off her clothes.

She slipped her fingers up and traced the edge of his jaw. Keil shut his eyes to enjoy the sensations tingling through his blood. She wiggled and he looked down to see she was shaking silently, tears trickling from her eyes.

"Hey, it's okay." He tilted her head back to reassure her and stopped at the expression on her face.

Sheer delight.

"What's up, little bird?"

Robyn wiped at her eyes and crawled off his lap, stopping only to plant a kiss on his cheek. She returned to his side with her notepad, dragging up another chair so they could face each other but both still enjoy the fire's warmth.

It may seem insane but I'm so happy right now, she wrote.

"Happy? Having to rescue my brother makes you happy? Leaving him buried for once would make me ecstatic."

Her snort of laughter made him smile.

"Tell me, how can having your whole world turned upside down make you happy?"

Robyn stared at him for a minute then bent her head to write. When she handed him the note pad, she signaled like she was drinking from a glass.

He turned to read her message as she went to the water bucket.

All my life I've been different. But it's been bad different. It's hard to share with new people. My only friends my brother and old family friends.

But you accept me right away. You trust me right away. Your brother is an idiot right away! You're real with me.

All that makes me very happy.

Keil lifted his head to see her watching him with her big brown eyes, a soft smile on her lips.

"You have been different. It's because you were supposed to be a wolf. You were supposed to be around your pack who would love you and support you. That's what's been missing." He took the glass she held to him and placed it to the side with care before pulling her back into his arms.

"I won't rush you, and you probably still have a ton of questions but, you need to know that I'll do anything for you. The connection between us is growing stronger, and I'm glad that I've found you." He leaned down and kissed her.

Soft. Gentle. A kiss of exquisite tenderness. He put his heart into the motion, trying to tell her without words that she didn't have to worry about him, and that all the concerns of the day would work out fine in the end.

"How can I feel this connected with someone I just met?"

Keil froze.

He'd heard her voice in his mind.

Pulling back, he stared into her eyes. He thought it would happen, but not already. They weren't even mates yet. She hadn't had her wolf triggered.

It was impossible.

"How did you do that?" he asked.

Her expression grew puzzled, and he tried to paste on a smile. It must have not worked because she pulled away.

"Wait, try something for me. Tell me your favorite colour."

After giving him the "are you insane" look she did oh-so-well, she reached for the notepad.

"No writing. Try and tell me in my head."

Robyn stared at him. *"He's doing the crazynut thing again. I don't have a favorite colour to tell him."*

"Everyone has a favorite colour, Robyn."

Her face went pale. *"Did you hear me?"*

Keil stroked her cheek and attempted to speak to her mind. *"Yup, it goes well with the 'crazynut thing' that I do."*

She scrambled off his lap, ending up in a pile on the floor.

"Holy shit! You can hear me. I can hear you! How is this possible?" She pulled herself up to her knees and grabbed his legs. Then she dragged herself upright until they were eye-to-eye. *"Say something else to me."*

"You're the most beautiful thing I've ever seen."

She blew a raspberry at him. *"Say something intelligent."*

Instead he dove at her, trailing kisses over her lips and flowing down the edge of her neck to bury his face in the V of her shoulder. *"You're beautiful and you smell like a spring meadow. Your skin feels fresh and clean like the wind blowing over the glacier. You taste like a fresh-caught fish with a good glass of wine."*

"You poet, you. You're making me hungry."

Keil lifted his head and stared into her eyes. *"You make me hungry too, and I'm planning on doing something about it. I wanted to wait but..."*

Her fingers laced into the hair at the back of his neck. *"This is crazy. My body feels like I'm on fire. How can I hear you? You said this morning that mates could sometimes speak like this but we're not mates. I mean, doesn't that require us to have sex first?"*

"It usually does. The only thing I can think of is the adrenaline rush from the avalanche triggered you and started to link us. Life and death situation, and all that. You're an exceptionally strong wolf, and so am I. Not that I'm bragging or anything."

Robyn blinked at him. He grinned back as he stood, lifted her and took a step toward the sleeping platform. He stopped and checked around the room. Shaking his head he turned back, his need for her growing stronger.

"Damn, I want you. But not here. Get your things together."

"We're going to have sex? Now?"

She was thinking so hard he could hear the echo of her concern bounce off the mountainside. *"Now. And if that means we not only trigger your wolf, we get you pregnant at the same time, we'll hold a double celebration. You're my mate. That means lots of great sex and a family to boot. Whenever it happens, sooner or later. You have any trouble with that?"*

Her shy head shake almost undid him.

7

$\mathcal{R}$obyn shifted uncomfortably on the bench in the annex outside the sauna. Keil had gone back to the cabin with TJ and left her with the directions to relax and wait for him while he grabbed a few things.

She added a couple extra logs into the stove, topped up the snow in the buckets and sat to wait.

It was damn uncomfortable to be sitting there knowing any moment a werewolf was going to walk in the door and have sex with her.

Arghhhh. Even the thought made her twitch. What the hell was she doing? This was crazy. It was beyond crazy.

The door opened, and she jumped. Sexual heat flowed off his body and reached to caress her.

Okay. She remembered why she was going to do this. Every inch of her was on fire and she was being drawn toward the tall, hard male as if she had ropes that twined about her limbs, trapping her.

Keil dropped a blanket on the bench beside her. He checked her expression before lifting her chin with his hand.

"Hey, it's okay. We'll take this slowly."

Robyn dropped her eyes, blushing furiously as she spoke into his mind. *"I'm scared."*

"Scared of me?"

"Kind of."

His gentle hand traced over her ear and nestled in the hair at the back of her neck. *"I don't want to scare you. I want to love you."*

She lifted her eyes to his. *"I don't know what to do. I mean, I know what to do, but I've never..."*

Keil waggled his eyebrows and his eyes brightened. "I know you've never. I'm glad you've never. It's good that you've never. Now I don't have to go track down your old lovers to kill them."

"Possessive much?"

"You have no idea. Yet." He leaned closer to brush his lips over hers. *"Wait until you're fully wolf. I bet you'll be just as possessive about me. Wolves mate for life, and we don't like to share."*

Robyn shifted on the hard bench. How could she want this much yet still feel afraid to take the next step?

She closed her eyes and took a deep breath, trying to build up her courage.

A gentle touch pulled her to her feet. *"You're thinking too hard. Let's go slow. You must be sweaty from our ski and digging up TJ. Let me help wash you up."*

His hands drifted over her shoulders, pulling her against his body for a brief caress as he reached behind her to grasp the bottom of her long-sleeved T-shirt. With a slow fluid motion, he lifted it off, then dropped it on the bench behind them.

As his eyes traced over her torso, Robyn fought the urge to cover her chest with her hands. Ugh. She had to decide to be seduced in a mountain cabin wearing her plainest and sturdiest underwear.

Luckily, he didn't express any displeasure with what he saw.

And neither could she complain. Keil removed his own shirt with one swift yank and stood inches away from her, his rock-solid stomach tempting her fingers.

"Damn. Just...damn. Is that what they mean by washboard abs? Can I do some laundry?"

He smiled and reached for her. Removing the tight sports bra didn't go as smoothly. In the middle of pulling it off, his hand got stuck in the twist of the Y back, and she froze with her arms pulled over head, bra wrapping her tight with his forearm. Heat rose to her face.

"Hell of a thing to happen, but don't worry. This gives us some very interesting possibilities." He lowered his head to press his lips to her neck. He fluttered soft kisses over the tops of her exposed breasts, sending chills shooting through her even as he supported and stretched her arms above them.

His touch was gentle, but the restrained power was there, under the surface. His tongue stroked toward her cleavage then his teeth nibbled back up the line of heat he'd created all the way to her lips.

His hand was loose from her bra and she lowered her arms slowly, his hot gaze never leaving her body.

"Take off the rest and I'll get the shower ready."

He spun away quickly, leaving Robyn wondering what she'd done wrong. *"Keil?"*

He answered even as his strong arms poured heated water into the holding tank over the top of the shower. *"I need to cool off a bit. You're very beautiful, and because you're my mate, I really, really want you. I'm trying to keep things slow here."*

After prepping the water, he placed her into the shower, turning her until she was wet from head to toe. With a flick of the wrist, he stopped the water and picked up the washcloth and soap.

Starting at the back of her neck, he rubbed small circles over her skin, covering her shoulder blades, slipping over her spine until his hands cupped both cheeks of her ass.

Robyn dropped her forehead against the side of the shower stall and closed her mind to everything but the wonderful sensations racing over her skin at his touch. The heat from the sauna warmed the side room they were in to the point that she was comfortable even as droplets continued to cling to her skin.

His mouth fastened on her neck, lapping at stray pebbles of water pooled there. Her sex clenched, releasing moisture as every stroke of his tongue sent thrills through her, desire rising deep inside.

His touch dropped lower as Keil squatted behind her, his hands caressing down one leg.

The small circular motions were driving her crazy as he teased, moving closer to the core of her heat and retreating without satisfying.

"Turn around, beautiful."

His voice in her mind was deep and dark, like rich chocolate. Robyn was so into chocolate.

His voice made the tingles race.

She pivoted to face him as he continued to kneel in front of the shower stall. She gazed down, shocked by the powerful look of need reflecting back.

He drew a shaky breath, dipped his washcloth into the

warm water he had by his side, and the torment began again.

Only now she could watch as well as feel his touch. He dropped his gaze over her as he washed her feet carefully before moving up her legs. She caressed his head, enjoying the erotic feel of his hair under her fingers.

Impulsively, she bent and loosened his ponytail holder, combing out the braid to let the dark strands pour over his shoulders in a fountain of dark silk.

His attention had reached the level of her pussy, and she drew in a sharp breath as he licked his lips and shot her a glance hot enough to make her melt. The cloth dipped, and this time Keil lifted it still dripping to softly touch her folds. The warm water ran over her skin, slipping into the crevices hidden from his eyes only to continue the journey down her legs in slow rivulets.

He dropped the cloth to the side and used both hands to open her to his gaze. Robyn shivered at the intimate touch. She closed her eyes only to have them shoot open at the feel of his tongue darting against the small nub he exposed.

"*Ohhh.*"

His mouth lowered on her, his tongue gentle as it slipped up and down the sides of her sex, each pass including a circle around the tip of her clitoris.

While one hand held her open, the fingers of the other dipped lower. He explored her pussy, tracing circles in the moisture he found.

"*Oh, babe, you are so damn beautiful. You may have never made love before, but your body knows what to do. Feel how wet you are? That's your body getting you ready for me. You're wet and hot and...*" his tongue dipped lower to thrust into her, "*...and oh-so-tasty.*"

Robyn was sure she was going to collapse. She shook as the assault on her pussy continued. Keil raised one of her legs and placed it over his shoulder, opening her even more to his touch.

He pressed back on her torso until she leaned on the shower wall, then shifted his hands to support her hips.

With that single motion she was held in his grasp, completely at his mercy. He increased the tempo of his mouth, licking and caressing every inch of her pussy, his hot breath bathing her limbs. The tension inside her was rising, closer and closer to exploding, when one hand dropped back down. He slipped a finger into her passage and stroked in and out.

"Does it feel good? I want you to enjoy this."

Robyn tried to engage her brain enough to answer, but it was impossible. She was a puddle of warm goo, and if he wasn't careful, she was going to slip down the drain. The tingles had been replaced by electrical zaps that could power a small village, and she was panting hard enough she was in danger of hyperventilating.

A second finger joined the first, and the feeling of fullness countered with the exquisite torture on her clit sent her over a cliff with an explosion that knocked her off her remaining leg. Supported only by his hands and the wall behind her, her body squeezed hard around his fingers, moisture drenching him as his tongue continued to lap at her.

"Hmmm, you don't need to answer. I know you liked that. You're delicious." He kissed a trail up to her bellybutton, then stood her on her feet.

His tender touch supported her until she stopped swaying. He flicked on the tap, and the warm water of the shower slid over her skin.

Soft, gentle caresses over her back rinsed away the soap he'd used earlier.

As the water stopped, Robyn opened her eyes to stare directly into his face.

Heat and deep need shone back at her.

Wrapping his arms around her, Keil lifted her, carrying her into the sauna, leaving the door open behind them. He sat on the widest bench and arranged her on his lap facing him.

Kisses like a ten-car pile-up were followed by his hands soft and gentle over her breasts. Her head fell back as he palmed one breast and lowered his mouth to the other, lapping and suckling at the needy tip until it hardened to a peak.

He switched his attention to the other side, each tug of his mouth sending another streak of desire from her nipple to her core, tension building as her desire for him grew stronger.

He smelled good. He felt even better.

She let her fingers wander over his shoulders and down his torso as he made love to her breasts. Slipping her fingers through his hair, she felt the connection between them growing tighter, more concentrated. Tendrils of emotion, not only desire, but affection and friendship, wrapped around her.

More than sex. They were definitely making love.

Robyn lifted her head to stare at him. He sat back and leaned against the wall. His eyes were full of raw emotion.

It was all too amazing. Almost overwhelming. *"Did you feel that? That was... Wow."*

"I felt it. Wow is right. Your turn. I need you to touch me."

He took her hand, guiding it to where his cock stood

rigid between their bodies. He was so hard the swollen head tapped his belly, a drop of moisture clinging to the small slit.

She stroked softly, velvet over steel.

His eyes closed, and a shiver ran through his body.

Robyn swallowed hard. She used both hands to explore, trying not to freak out at how big he was. *"Umm, Keil? I think I'm afraid again. No way will this thing fit in me. Ugh. I've read that in stories before, and it sounded stupid, but seriously, you are hung like a damn horse."*

Laughter shook his body. *"And in all the stories you've read, does the 'thing' fit?"*

"Yes, but—"

"No butts. Not today." His strong hands slapped her ass gently. *"We'll save that for another time."*

"Now you're really scaring me!"

He lay on the bench and made her straddle his body, his cock pressed hard along the cheeks of her ass. His hands continued to smooth over her. Dipping and gliding over her back, her breasts, her belly.

Each stroke raised her temperature as tremors grasped her.

He touched her clit, making small circles along the wet lips of her pussy until he pushed her over the edge into another orgasm.

When her breath was halfway back to normal, Keil lifted her hips and supported her over the tip of his cock.

She took her weight onto her knees and he used one hand to rub the wet head of his shaft against her pussy lips again and again.

"Ride me. Go as slow as you want."

She joined her hand to his as he directed his cock into her warmth. She checked his face before she moved, tenderness reflected in his eyes along with need and desire.

She pressed down, freezing as the head of his shaft stretched her wide. The sides of her passage were wet, and excitement blurred her senses.

"I...think it feels good."

"Little bit more, babe. I promise it will feel great."

They were barely moving, more forward and back than up and down, but every tiny pulse of her hips fed the fire building in her belly until she zigged instead of zagging.

His cock slipped deeper, and a shot of pain cracked through the haze of desire, and she hesitated.

"Keil?"

"Lean forward, and let me have those beautiful lips for a minute."

His mouth met hers, and she tangled their tongues together, letting him regain control of her hips as he continued to rub against her.

He licked from the corner of her mouth to her neck, and her brain shut down. He suckled at her skin then put his teeth to her.

One solid thrust with his hips drove him through her barrier to rest deep inside. Simultaneously he bit down on her neck and the joint pleasure/pain of the two piercings flashed through her body, her inner walls clutched at his cock, her hands tangled in his hair.

"Sweet mercy, what have you done to me?"

He pulled her torso against his body and held her tight, waiting as she adjusted to his girth stretching her.

The feel of his hard body under her hands, the beating of his heart mixed with the pleasure still tingling through her washed away the remnants of pain.

Slowly he began to move, pulling her hips high enough the tip of his cock clung to her entrance, then lowering her all the way down, angling to go as deep as possible.

Robyn pushed her body upright so she could watch, one hand pressed to his chest, one hand dropping to feel where they connected to each other.

The intimacy of touching his cock, having it brush along her fingers as it slipped into her body made her head spin with delight.

Keil smiled up at her and added his hand to hers, linking fingertips, rubbing her clit with each drive of his hips.

She pressed down in tempo with his thrusts, needing him to go faster, go deeper. The air from the sauna around them seemed to cool as their bodies warmed to boiling, passion driving higher and higher until she climaxed once more, her sex clenching tight around his cock as he joined her, the warmth of his seed bathing her with fire deep inside.

～

HE CLUNG TO HER, holding tight until the tremors subsided.

Limbs tangled, Robyn's head resting on his chest, Keil felt the tendrils of connection complete and settle into his soul.

His mate.

He stroked one hand over her hair, brushing the strands off her face to stare at her. Her bright eyes were filled with a touch of bewilderment and a whole lot of satisfaction.

Her full lips were wet from where she'd licked them, and he found himself hardening at the thought of leaning down to nuzzle her mouth.

Not yet, he told himself sternly. *"How are you?"*

"That was...well actually, that was amazing. If I'd

known it was going to be this much fun I'd have tried it sooner." A frown crossed her face. *"Keil? Are you growling at me? I can feel the vibrations."*

He pulled back the anger that had flashed through him at the thought of anyone touching her.

"Sorry, love, under control now. How about we go again if you enjoyed it that much? Or try a few other things?"

"Not the butt, wolfman. You're not going there. What should we do about TJ, though? He's sitting in the cabin all alone."

He lifted her and carried her back to the shower, gently rinsing the signs of their lovemaking off her limbs. He couldn't resist caressing her pussy softly and stirring her fires again.

"Actually, TJ isn't in the cabin anymore. I told him to go home. He may not be able to ski by himself, but since the silly boy lost all his equipment in the accident, he'll have to run home as a wolf anyway. We'll meet him in Haines Junction at the condo the pack owns. The cabin is all ours. Welcome to our honeymoon suite."

Robyn touched his cheek and pulled him into the shower stall with her. She picked up the cloth to wash his chest, teasing down his happy trail and making his mind turn to mush.

"That's the best news I've heard in a while. Keil?"

He'd closed his eyes as her fingers traced over his shaft, one hand stopping to cup his balls, the other slipping from side to side over the sensitive skin on the head.

"Yes?"

"It fit. It fit just fine."

8

$\mathcal{K}$eil managed to keep one hand tucked around her even as he finished scooping up the rest of the noodles from the dinner pot.

He never seemed to be far away. He touched her constantly. Over the past three days, they had made love in the sauna, in the cabin, even enjoyed a quick romp on the porch under the moonlight.

One night he'd eaten a piece of cheesecake off her belly, then proceeded to lick every inch of her thoroughly before taking her quivering body to the shower house to continue.

When they weren't making love they skied, built a snow fort and talked for hours about everything.

Robyn couldn't decide whether she liked the talking or the loving better. Being with Keil was amazing. There were definitely benefits to this mate thing.

"It's only Tuesday but I think we should ski out tomorrow like TJ and I had planned. There's a lot we need to do before Saturday."

She nodded hesitantly.

"*What, little bird?*"

She pressed her lips against his cheek. "*I don't want to go home yet. This is the shortest honeymoon on record.*"

"*Oh, the honeymoon isn't over, sweetie. We'll have to delay the rest until after...*" He broke off, his body tensing up next to hers.

Robyn stood to clear away the dishes, fighting to keep tears at bay.

The pack challenge. She understood from their talks that it had to happen, but she wasn't ready to share him yet. With anyone.

He swung her to face him, speaking into her mind, a smooth caress of love accompanying the words.

"*This is not how I would have chosen to make you my mate, forcing changes on you this quickly. But we needed each other. I needed you. I won't apologize for taking advantage of finding you and loving you.*"

Her heart pounded at his affirmation of love. "*Oh, Keil.*"

"*You're going to have your first full moon as a wolf on Saturday, and the challenge isn't until Sunday. Come back to Haines with me. I'll introduce you to the pack members who support me. I will win the challenge. Especially now that I have you. Trust me.*"

"*I do trust you, but I can't go to Haines. I'm supposed to phone my brother today because he plans to meet me on Saturday at the trailhead. I have to talk to him if there's any changes, and this is going to be tough to explain. Oh, hell.*"

He looked puzzled for a minute. "You said you had a satellite phone. How were you planning on using it? You can't hear."

"*Text message.*"

"On a sat phone?"

"Ain't technology great?"

"I'd hate to know what that costs per message. Can I talk to your brother for you?"

Robyn considered. Tad was the kind to worry, but he also knew when to back down. She thought Keil would be able to talk it out with her brother.

It might, however, take a while. *"Only if you plan on paying the charges."*

"What are you, cheap?"

"Like borscht."

He pulled her in for a kiss, the kind that made her toes curl and her heartbeat increase.

Just as it was getting interesting, he broke it off. *"Damn, you get tastier and tastier. I'd better make that call before I get too distracted. What's the number?"*

She pulled out the phone and handed him one of Tad's business cards that she kept with it.

Keil choked for a second before flashing a big grin.

What was the damn wolf up to now? The expression in his eyes was way too mischievous.

He linked the call through then sat back to talk, making sure she could see his lips.

"Hi, Tad, this is Keil Lynus. How are you, man?" He winked at her, and a warning signal went off in her brain. Something stunk. "No, TJ doesn't need any rescuing, we already dug him out... I know, he's a total pain in the butt. I do need something... She's fine. In fact, Robyn and I are mates, and I was—"

She stared in shock. How could he blurt it out like that to Tad? Her brother must be freaking. She slapped at Keil's shoulder, trying to take the phone away from him.

"Hang on, Tad, she's getting a little frisky right now. I

think she's worried you're having a fit or something over there. Want to talk to her?"

With a violent yank she stole the phone away from him to check the screen. Maybe he hadn't phoned anyone at all and it was a joke.

But there was a return message on the screen.

Tad: *Congratz, sis, Keil is awesome. I'm happy for u*

Her jaw dropped to the floor. She typed in quickly: *U know Keil? U know what he is?*

Tad: *Ya. Wolf. u work fast sis*

Robyn: *U are so dead next time I c u*

Tad: *luv U 2*

Robyn: *Jerk*

Keil pulled the phone away, said "hi" and paused to listen for a minute.

"Well, thanks. It was a surprise, but she's incredible, Tad. Hey, there's a little thing shaking down this weekend if you'd like to join us. Robyn's first full moon will be on Saturday... Of course you can come! You're family, even if you aren't triggered yet... I know, Tad." Keil rolled his eyes. "It'll happen sometime, man. Gotta go. Robyn's making me pay for this call... Of course I can afford it, but why would I want to spend more time talking to you when I can be with my mate?"

She fought to control her breathing as Keil hung up and packed away the phone. The smirk on his face was more than she could handle, and she pounded on his arm.

"Hey, what's this? I thought that went rather well. Tad will even be able to join us for the full moon. Great, hey?"

"You ass. You never told me you knew my brother. How does he know you, and how come he knew you were a wolf, and—"

He wrapped his arms around her and lifted her off her feet as she continued to struggle against him.

Robyn fumed. Keil had known Tad all along? That meant Tad knew about werewolves and never once said anything to her about the fact she was one.

Good grief. That was probably the "big secret" he'd kept trying tell her.

They were both dead.

Keil lowered her to the sleeping platform and covered her body with his own, stopping her from wiggling away. The thrill of his touch battled with the desire to kick his kneecaps off.

"Tell me what's up, or I'll be forced to hurt you."

"You'd never hurt me."

"Oh yeah? Ever eaten a granola bar with a laxative additive? I can arrange it."

He laughed and rolled to the side, running a hand over her body as he spoke. "I didn't realize the connection when you said you were a Maxwell. You told me you had a brother, but you never told me his name."

Robyn opened her mouth to protest then froze. *"Damn. Are you sure?"*

He nodded. "I would have recognized the name. I know Tad from my guiding business. He flies us on trips all the time. He told me he had a sister, but he never said she was deaf. He found out we were wolves on a trip when TJ did one of his not-so-amazing Houdini tricks while Tad was still around.

"I'm going to kill him," she announced.

"Your brother is a half-breed wolf, still untriggered. We guessed it was your Grampa who gave him the genes. If you're wondering, yes, he knew you were a wolf." She tensed under his hands. "Hey, think of it this way. He can't shift until he gets triggered, and that's complicated for a male half-breed. Telling you about werewolves wasn't going to work because he had no proof. He probably thought your mate would be someone from one of the Whitehorse packs."

Robyn dropped her head back on the bunk with a flash of insight. "Is that why he's been introducing me to all these different 'clients' over the years? Were they all wolves?"

"Maybe. He did mean well, remember that before you slit his throat, my vengeful hussy." He slid his hands over her possessively. *"Since it's our last night here I vote we take advantage of it. Dinner was great, but I want my dessert."*

He opened her shirt and proceeded to bury his head in her breasts, rubbing back and forth over her torso like he was painting himself with her scent.

"You can't tell, but you smell absolutely amazing. It's something to do with being recently triggered as well as being my mate, but your pheromones are off the chart right now." He licked a long slow line up from between her breasts until he reached her lips and proceeded to tease the corners of her mouth with gentle nips and kisses.

"TJ said it could be a problem with the pack. That all the guys would be attracted to me."

Keil pulled back and stared at her for a second. "He's right, I never thought about that. I mean, you're marked as mine, and your scent is clearly our scent, but as a full-blood until after your first full moon, you're sending off killer hormones."

He traced a finger down her body, circling the globes of her breasts as he considered. "I'll be careful who I introduce you to. Only mated couples and females until after the weekend. You're too beautiful. I'd be fighting everyone for you otherwise."

"You wolves seem to like fighting."

"It passes the time and keeps us warm. It's cold in Alaska."

Robyn grabbed his hand from where it teased her and pushed it farther down her body until his strong fingers cupped her mound. She pressed her hips upward gently, encouraging him to explore. *"It's cold in the Yukon too, but I know of lots of other ways to stay warm. Fireplaces, hot tubs..."*

"...saunas, beds. I'm looking forward to trying them all with you." He spread his fingers over her belly and finally lowered his head to her breast. His tongue flicked out to moisten the tip of her nipple. Her body responded and a tight peak formed.

His contented smile warmed her heart. He didn't simply go through the motions. He seemed to enjoy touching her, making her feel wonderful.

He blew a stream of cool air over her breast, sending a shot of pleasure down to her womb. Slowly he lowered his mouth until he could suck the erect tip into his mouth, tugging sharply. He followed with a gentle lap. A delicate nip with his teeth.

The alternating tugs and soft caresses built up the pressure burning deep in her core. She reached her hands to massage over his shoulders, holding him close to her body.

Suddenly she needed more. She wanted to touch him, make him feel as good as he made her feel. He'd been such a tender lover over the past days, but he'd been controlling as well, never letting her take charge.

"...oh damn, that feels good. I want you to roll over. Please?"

She felt his chuckle against her breast. *"You going somewhere, little bird?"* His mouth continued to feast as he pulled her into his arms and flipped them over, finishing with her nestled on top.

He was still sucking.

Robyn tucked up her legs to straddle his strong body, giving her leverage. She slowly lifted her torso away from his caresses.

The expression of loss on his face made her smile. *"It's okay, wolfman, I'm not going anywhere but down."*

His puzzled expression faded as heat flared in his eyes. She winked and started the exploring she wanted to do.

His body was amazing, and all hers to enjoy. Taut chest muscles that flexed under her hands, nipples that tightened as she stroked over their tips. He seemed to enjoy her touch there as much as she had enjoyed his.

She lowered her mouth to lick gently at the erect tip.

His body jerked. Yup, he liked it too. Robyn copied his earlier example and blew. Another body jerk followed.

"You're killing..."

She moved farther south, lapping the edges of the six-pack that had impressed her since their first night together, the ridges sharp and defined as his muscles clenched with anticipation.

"Please..."

Robyn slid between his thighs as she descended his body. She paused, resting on her elbows, to examine him in all his glory.

His erect cock saluted her from only inches away. The head had turned a deep purple shade, a bead of moisture shining on the slit. The thick top sloped sharply to the rigid shaft.

She used just the tip of her tongue. Soft, tentative.

"Holy..."

Robyn flicked a glance up to see his dark eyes flashing at

her. She liked that he was unable to complete full sentences. She liked the way his body responded to her touch. She must be doing something right.

Heat poured off him, and the scent of raw sex in the air was driving her wild. She grinned, and maintaining eye contact, sucked the head of his cock into her mouth.

His eyes rolled back in his head and his six-pack tightened further. If that was possible.

She fell into a rhythm, a swirl of her tongue over the edge of the rim followed by an attempt to take as much of him into her mouth as possible.

The first couple of times she gagged a little as the crown of his cock hit the back of her throat, but the wetter her mouth got, the easier it was to slip him past her lips even as he grew harder. Thicker.

Her excitement grew as well. Touching Keil, pleasuring him like this, turned her on big time, getting her all hot and bothered. She closed her eyes and hummed with delight.

"Damn it, that's enough. I'm not wasting this."

His powerful arms lifted her and he swung her around, finishing with his body pressed hard to her back. His cock nestled between her legs, and Robyn instinctively threw out her arms to brace her body before it could hit the mattress.

"I was enjoying myself! I wanted to make you feel good."

"Babe, I feel great. But I don't want to come in your mouth tonight. I want your hot, tight body to squeeze me. I want to feel you around me when you come. Tonight is for both of us. Now, open your legs wider."

He smoothed a hand over her hip and pressed her body lower to the mattress, exposing her more clearly to his gaze.

"Damn, you are beautiful. Everywhere. Like a flower opening up to me." He shifted his body away, letting his fingers dip into her passage. He touched his wet fingers to

the tight rosebud hidden between her cheeks. She stiffened, uncertain if she wanted to wiggle away or press closer to the exploring finger that circled, touched. Teased.

"Whoa, I'm not sure about that."

"Hush. I'm not going to do anything you won't like. Someday I'm going to take you in the ass, but not today. Today I'll show you something special. Trust me."

His hands were everywhere. Slipping over her breasts, tweaking her nipples to hard needy peaks before swirling over her belly and pressing intimately against her clit

A finger slid inside her, stroked a few times then withdrew, leaving her feeling empty. Then he started all over.

Robyn pressed her hips back, trying to make contact with his body. *"No more teasing. I need you. Please."*

Suddenly he was there, skin-to-skin with her, his hard, hot cock against her core. Keil leaned forward and his mouth latched onto her shoulder. He sucked hard, his teeth pressing the skin. He covered the place where he'd marked her earlier, and as he sucked, a bolt of lightning flashed through her and set off an orgasm that she swore shook the cabin.

And the mountain. Possibly the entire territory, but she could be mistaken about that.

Then he surged into her in one smooth motion that set off another explosion that registered on the Richter scale.

Damn, he was good.

He set up a smooth pace, burying his entire length deep inside her on every thrust, his balls slamming against her. He held her hips firmly and used them to pull her back onto him as his speed picked up.

"I've wanted you like this since the beginning. You can't know how much it turns me on to see you in front of me,

spread for my pleasure, your breasts swaying. You're so hot and wet and tight around me. Your ass is beautiful, smooth and inviting." He shifted one hand to run over the sensitive nerves of her anus, dipping a finger past the rim even as he continued to pump into her with his cock.

Her body was on overload. She hadn't come down from the last climax, and every nerve in her body tingled. Her breasts rubbed the sleeping bag every time he entered her. His shaft seemed to grow in size as his finger pressed even farther into her ass in time with the thrusts of his cock. The double penetration made her grow wetter than ever as all the sensations drew to another peak. The unending in and out strokes built heat where she thought there was nothing left to burn.

His free hand slipped around her to touch her clit, and she screamed, the wildfire ripping through her consuming every available inch of skin and tissue.

He slammed into her one last time and she felt the flood of warmth from his release, felt the hard length within her jerk again and again as his hands locked them together.

It was hours later, she was sure of it, before she had enough energy to even draw a breath of air into her lungs. Her body tingled from top to bottom, although she had to admit that the bottom area tingled a bit more than anywhere else.

He reluctantly pulled away from her, and she mourned the loss. She was resting on the platform trying to catch her breath, head down and butt up in the air, when a soft warm cloth slipped over her. Keil cleaned her up with such a gentle touch she wasn't even sure he was there the whole time.

When he was done he picked her up and held her close, settling in front of the fire. She slipped a hand over his jaw and smiled at him. His dark eyes stared down, the heat of passion still there, but something else as well. Something gentle and deep and forever.

Robyn laid her head against his chest. She swore that she heard his heart beating.

For her.

Only for her.

9

The ski out with Keil was a hoot. He didn't take the straight route down the hills, instead veering off into the trees and making teleturns as often as possible.

Just like Robyn liked to do.

Usually it drove Tad crazy, but here was her mate doing the same insane thing. It felt great, and it was tons of fun to have someone to ski with who didn't freak out every time she left the main trail.

They made it down to the level of the second lake after an hour. The small hunter's cabin at the head of the lake was in disrepair, but still a great place to stop for a hot drink and a short snack.

They were putting their gear back in their packs and getting ready for the ski across the lake when she threw her arms around Keil and hugged him, hard. She was incredibly happy she could talk with him. Usually having to use sign language and read lips made the outward journey disjointed, but because of the magic of being mates, she could talk to him anytime.

She wondered how far away from each other they could be and still hear each other.

He brushed her arm, amusement on his face. *"What's up?"*

No use in being shy about it. *"I love being with you. I love being able to speak into your mind and hear you in mine. I love skiing with you."*

"I love skiing with you too. Especially that little trick you have of squealing with delight before skiing over steep embankments."

Robyn hit him with a hastily formed snowball. *"I do not squeal."*

His gaze dropped over her body and heat rolled between them. *"You most certainly do squeal. And moan. And make all sorts of other delicious noises. Hell, I'm hard just thinking about it. Wanna fool around?"*

She lifted a brow. *"It's twenty-five degrees out, and we're in the middle of the forest. Cool your jets."*

The leer he gave her as he reached down and adjusted himself promised some serious torture in the very near future. *"Do you realize how tough it is going to be to travel like this?"*

"Put a ski on it. You'll be the fastest thing on three legs."

She danced away from him, laughing, and readied for the two-hour journey across the lake.

The snow pack was beautiful. Hard snow covered the surface with a heavy enough dusting of fresh powder to give their skis something to bite into.

Once again Keil led the way, setting tracks for her to follow. They continued to talk back and forth to each other easily about nothing in particular, avoiding discussing the pack, the challenge, everything controversial.

Robyn enjoyed the rapid pace he set, and she was

disappointed when he slowed down, glancing into the trees on their right.

"*Hey, you getting tired or something?*"

"*Or something. Keep skiing, but reduce your speed. Keep your eyes on my back. Understand?*"

"*No. We need to pick it up, or we'll be in Haines in a week instead of a day.*"

"*Are you watching my back?*"

She ran her eyes over the solid body in front of her. Her mouth watered at the thought he was all hers.

"*Your backside. Does that count? Yummy.*"

"*Glad you think so. Don't freak out, but I think we're being shadowed. I count at least four wolves in the trees beside us. Are you still watching me?*"

A shiver raced through her. Something was very wrong, or he would have simply stopped and faced the wolves. "*I'm watching you. What's happening?*"

"*I think someone is trying to pull a fast one. If the other challenger to the Alpha position can take me out ahead of time, they can assume leadership. They must think you're TJ. People knew he was going to Granite with me.*"

"*Yuck, what an insult. Have they never seen him ski?*" Her indignation vanished as the rest of what he'd said sank in. "*Wait, what do you mean 'take you out'? Are they going to attack us?*"

Keil continued to ski forward, Robyn narrowing the gap between them as his pace slowed.

She slipped a couple of furtive glances toward the trees and spotted some of the wolves darting in and out of the distant tree line.

"*Yeah, they're going to attack.*" He somehow managed to sound reassuring in her mind. "*Listen up. They don't know we're mates, which means they don't know we can talk like this. That's to our advantage. If Jack were to do this right, he'd approach me alone, and his seconds would stand back and watch. By sneaking up on us out here, I doubt Jack's planning on obeying any of the rules."*

"Bastards." She was scared, but pissed off as well.

"If they think you're TJ, they're going to assume you'll fight like him." Keil paused. *"For all that he's clumsy and an annoyance, TJ's a tough wolf. I'm guessing they will set two wolves on you."*

"Two wolves? That's not good odds, but if we stick together—"

"I want to, but we'd never survive that way. A four against two means they can actually have three against one at times, and even I can't fight that many at once without getting hurt. The thought is killing me, but I'm going to have to leave you for a bit."

She hadn't realized it was possible to send a gasp through mind speak.

Keil hurried on. *"I'll attack the two that go after me, get at least one of them out of the picture, then rejoin you. I told you about wolf society and ranking. You're strong enough to hold them off."*

They skied a bit farther as Robyn fought down her panic.

He was going to leave her and let two wolves attack her.

No, that wasn't true. He was going to trust her to defend herself until he could come back and save them both.

That sounded better. Even if it still made her want to pee her pants.

"Right around this bend the wind usually blows the snow off the lake. The ice will be a better surface for you to stand on to defend yourself. We'll ski until we get there."

She didn't know if she wanted the ski to be over, or to go on forever.

Finally Keil lifted a hand as if signaling for a rest stop. He shifted his body to face the trees, casually turning her toward him.

He undid his clothes while hiding from the view of the trees behind her body. A dangerous gleam lit his eyes, and an impression of power rolled off him. They might be in a tough place, but he was not going to be as easy a target as the others imagined.

"Protect your throat," he told her. "If they're close enough to get at your throat, I want you to shove your arm into their mouth. They'll still be able to snap it, and it'll hurt like hell, but your wolf can heal a busted arm. You can't regrow your throat."

Robyn gaped at him. *"Love you too, sweetheart. Man, you take your girl on the most romantic dates, don't you? Any other advice for me, Cujo?"*

Keil flashed a grin. "Just remember that kicking a wolf in the nuts hurts as much as it does a human."

"Good to know. So don't piss me off anymore, okay? What do you expect me to do, other than stand around looking like dinner?"

His answering smile reassured her more than it should have with wolves about to streak across the snow to try to kill her. "I expect you to use your ski poles, your big knife, and your tough-as-nails attitude, and kick some butt for me. Ready?"

"You're sexy when you're all tough. I guess if they think I'm TJ I shouldn't lean over and plant a big one on your cheek right now, hmmm?"

Keil threw back his head and laughed. His arms reached

out and while he kept his eyes on the tree line he kissed her thoroughly.

"What a wonderful idea. Now they're going to be worried about the sneak attack and freaking out watching us. Here they come. By the way, I do love you."

They drew a hands span apart. Keil threw off his clothes and shifted to his wolf. An instant later his silver grey form was racing toward the nearest of the wolves on the left. He flew across the snow, and she cheered inside as his huge body slammed into the first smaller wolf and bowled him over.

Then she couldn't watch anymore because the wolves on the right had closed in on her.

She turned and crouched, making sure she had a firm grip on her knife. Her pack lay to the side, and she made a mental note of its position to avoid tripping.

Glancing back up toward the trees, she gasped. *"Damn it, you owe TJ an apology. They obviously think he's tougher than you realized. There are* three *wolves coming at me."*

"I know. I've got three as well. Give me a second. Try and distract them."

Robyn gritted her teeth. Distract them? *"What, you want me to do a cancan dance, or something?"*

Fear and anger battled within her. It was bad enough Keil was supposed to have to fight in the challenge this weekend. That at least was a time-honoured tradition, and involved the values of fair play. This was nothing more than a sneak attack, cowardly and cheap.

She pulled the can of bear spray from her pocket where it had been stored since the start of the trip. One of the rules of the north was to never piss off anything you couldn't reason with.

Robyn was really pissed off.

She waited until the first wolf was in range, then lunged toward him as she held her breath and coated the beast with pepper spray.

A four-second burst was enough to set him howling in pain, scratching at his eyes with his paws as he rolled away from the fight, burying his face in the snow.

Dropping her knife and the bear spray, she reached down to grab the straps of her pack. She swung in a circle then let the pack fly into the next wolf, knocking him off his feet as she quickly retrieved her knife from the ground.

The remaining wolf was examining her, his head tilted to the side like he was thinking really hard.

Like he was really confused about something.

A quick glance toward Keil showed her he'd taken one wolf to the ground. His huge silver wolf body connected with another smaller black wolf, and the two of them rolled in the snow, scratching at each other's torsos and necks with their claws.

"Steady, Robyn, I'm on my way. Watch the black wolf on you. He's Jack's brother, and he's a mean one. The other wolf will try to distract you, but watch Dan."

Dan was still on the ground under the pack, but he'd lifted his head and was sniffing the air hard. He threw back his head and opened his mouth wide, and she assumed that he was howling.

Keil swore. *"Bloody hell. Run to me, NOW!"*

She turned, but Dan had regained his feet and lunged.

"I can't, he's attacking. What happened?"

"He's scented that you're my mate. He just told the others. Damn, I've got three on me again. Hold him off, babe, you can do it. He won't hurt you."

Robyn heard his anger even in her mind. Following

Dan's cry, the other wolf on her had left and he was attacking Keil, three on one again.

She jumped aside as Dan nipped at her legs. Her backhand swing was too slow to do more than brush her knife against his fur before he withdrew a short way. His wolf eyes mocked her as he herded her away from where her mate continued to fight.

Keil was stronger than any one of the wolves around him, but his attackers teased, dancing out of reach of his claws and teeth.

"What are they doing?"

"They're trying to drag out the fight. Tire me out before Jack even puts in an appearance."

Robyn pushed toward Keil, trying to narrow the gap between them, but she was frustrated time after time by Dan's lunges. She failed to see how close to the trees she'd been maneuvered.

Then she saw *him.*

Shit.

The new wolf was as big as Keil, black from tail to nose, and he walked out of the woods straight toward her fearlessly.

"Keil, who's this asshole?"

He risked a quick peek, and she felt his anger flare. *"That's the chief asshole himself. Jack."*

She couldn't keep her eyes on both Dan and Jack at the same time, and all at once, something slammed into the back of her legs and she fell, hard, to the ice. Swinging with her arm, she sliced hard with her knife and managed to hit meat this time. Only her arm went numb, and the blade flew from her fingers as her elbow was slammed to the ground by the weight of Jack's huge forepaw.

Her cry of distress reached Keil. *"Robyn, I'm coming. Hit him on the nose, kick him. Fight him."*

She tried not to freak out. Jack's massive body lay on top of her, pinning her to the ground

He sniffed along her ear.

"I can't move. He's at my throat and he's got my arms pinned. He must weigh five hundred pounds, and oh my word, that is gross."

"I'm almost there. What did he do?"

"He licked my neck. Gack, he stinks."

Robyn strained to pull her legs up to connect her feet with any part of Jack's anatomy. He continued to nuzzle along her throat, his tongue lapping occasionally as she struggled under him.

He didn't seem to be trying to hurt her, but the sheer weight of his body forced the air from her lungs. Between that and the smell of his breath, she was growing light-headed from a lack of oxygen.

Suddenly Keil was there, his massive body slamming into the side of Jack's body, and the two flew over her and rolled toward the scraggy trees.

Teeth flashed. Jack was no longer holding back as he had with Robyn. The fury of the attack, the speed of the swinging claws, made her gasp in horror.

Fur literally flew.

But even after having fought the other wolves, Keil was clearly stronger. His massive paws scrambled on the icy surface as he soon forced Jack down and over onto his back.

An instant later Keil placed his teeth against Jack's throat, setting his razor sharp claws on top of his opponent's belly.

He froze in position.

Waiting.

Robyn crawled crablike away from their fight, mesmerized. She slowly became aware that while she had waited nearby, the other wolves still standing had surrounded her.

"Oh crap."

"They won't touch you. I've got their leader in a death grip. Physically he's been defeated and acknowledged my superiority."

The wolves circled her slowly, taking small lunges in her direction. Moving closer on each rotation.

"Are you sure they know that? Because they're freaking me out here."

Keil's jaw moved, and she assumed he was talking to Jack. The black wolf threw back his head.

"Umm, Robyn? Slight problem. Remember TJ telling you about how being triggered made you smell kinda interesting right now?"

She sidestepped another wolf that had moved closer in an attempt to brush against her.

"Are you telling me these jerks have the hots for me?"

"Yup. We've got to convince them that you're already taken. Including Jack, who just made a comment about how good you taste, by the way."

The four wolves circling Robyn turned and began to slink toward Keil. Tails low, teeth bared, it was clear they planned on resuming the attack.

He pressed his paw more firmly into Jack's belly, but there was no way he could defend himself without releasing his captive.

"Call them off me," he ordered.

She ran up to one of the nearer wolves and kicked him in the flank. He simply rolled away and continued on his route toward Keil.

Desperately she tried to reach her mate's side, ignoring the pounding in her heart as she scrambled into the midst of six large wolves.

The males avoided her, intent on their target.

"They're not paying attention. I have no weapon left."

"Just call them off. You've got a powerful voice, and we're in the right here. It's our only chance. Do it now!"

Throwing herself against his side, she cried out, "Stop. Leave him alone."

All the wolves froze.

Heck, it was as if the entire world had frozen. A faint wind brushed her skin, but nothing else moved. The furry beasts gathered around them barely seemed to be breathing.

Robyn wasn't sure what had just happened.

Then Keil adjusted position, slowly withdrawing his paw and backing away from Jack.

He darted away, returning rapidly with his clothes and her knife. He had an extremely pleased expression on his wolfie face. *"You are damn beautiful. And that voice—mm, mm good."*

He shifted and dressed as he spoke, finishing off by grabbing her and continuing the kiss he'd started before the attack.

Was he out of his mind? *"Hello! Strange wolves loitering at our backs waiting to kill us, remember?"*

With a final gentle nip to her bottom lip, he reluctantly pulled away.

"You are so sexy when you use that Alpha voice. The puppies behind us? Take a look."

Robyn turned slowly.

All the wolves were lying belly down in the snow. When they saw her glance their way, they dropped their muzzles to the ground and covered their eyes with their front paws.

Jack, bloody from Keil's attack, crawled forward on his belly all the way to their feet. His dark eyes darted back and forth between them, then he slowly rolled to his back, exposing his throat.

Keil spoke aloud so the attackers could hear, sending the words to her as well. "Shall we kill them?"

She was a little shocked the idea didn't instantly repulse her. This being a wolf thing had definitely brought out the bloodthirsty part of her soul.

Still, there were other things to consider. *"Is the challenge still on for Sunday, or did your competition just disqualify himself?"*

"Oh, Jack is very much out of any challenge for Alpha. In fact, by the way they responded to your voice, I'd say you've shown we have complete power over any rebellious troublemakers from now on."

She dropped to her knees, pulling back sharply on Jack's ear, her knife close to his throat.

"Careful, babe. Think about it," Keil warned.

He was so sweet—trying to protect her. But in this case she had thought of the perfect plan for revenge.

The bastards had interrupted her honeymoon, after all. A little payback was in order.

"Oh, I know exactly what I want to do. I have only one thing to say to them."

A low buzz of amusement drifted across to her. The mental equivalent of a chuckle? *"Go ahead. I trust you."*

Robyn leaned closer to the ear she held tightly, and spoke clearly.

"Hey, asshole. Shift."

10

―――

"**S**he really made them shift?"

TJ, Tad and a few other close friends of Keil's sat together in one of the side rooms of the hall waiting for Robyn to appear. She was still getting ready for their entrance as the new Alphas for the pack and her first full moon.

"Oh, not only that, she made them stand around and introduce themselves. Butt-naked in the cold. Then they had to apologize to us both for 'disturbing the serenity of our honeymoon'."

He watched the ladies room door anxiously, adjusting the medallion around his neck again. If she didn't show up soon, he'd go pull her out.

"I thought Jack was going to pop a vein when she suggested he might like to look into purchasing one of the penis enhancers they advertise online."

Tad choked on his drink. "My sister?"

Keil exchanged knowing glances with TJ. "Oh, yeah. She's amazing. Don't piss her off any more than you usually do. Now that she's full wolf, she's a bit of a handful."

Tad sat back and swallowed hard.

Keil grinned at him. "Wait until she starts ordering you around."

"Are you getting me in trouble?"

He turned to face the door, eager for her to arrive. *"Of course not. You can get yourself in trouble all by yourself once you get here. Are you planning on arriving any time this century?"*

Scuffling noises on the other side of the door made him more hopeful than her words

"Look, oh tall and buff one, you only told me tonight there was going to be streaking involved in this shindig. I had to do a little more grooming than usual. Are you sure I have to get naked?"

The door opened and Robyn stepped through, dressed in the Alpha female's traditional pale blue robe. Her hair swung loose over her shoulders, and her eyes seemed to glow with the reflected light of the moon. Silver and gold and magical.

Keil's heart rose up and choked off his throat. The scent of her wolf increased as the moon drew nearer.

He'd been waiting for her all his life.

"Oh, yeah. You definitely have to get naked."

He turned up the hood on her robe, the soft white fur around the edge showing off her skin to perfection.

She pointed to the furry edge with an amused expression. *"The faux fur is hysterical, by the way, considering what we are."*

"When he was little, I had TJ convinced that was Great Grampa Stephen."

A laugh burst from her, drawing smiles from the crowd waiting behind them.

Then their eyes met again, heat rising rapidly. Desire

rolled over both of them as they stared at each other, the rest of the people in the room forgotten.

"Gag." TJ pretended to slip his finger down his throat. He slid in front of Robyn and kissed her cheek. "While I'm glad you're going to be my sister-in-law, and my Alpha, can you save the sex for when you get in front of the pack?"

Her face went completely white as she whipped around to glare at Keil. *"Is there any teeny, insignificant detail you might have forgotten to inform me about?"*

He shrugged and gave a look to let her know how much he wanted her. *"It may have slipped my mind. I don't think you'll mind—we'll be wolves. It's time to go."*

Keil held out his arm to lead her into the moonlight of the clearing.

Robyn paused for a second, and he offered up a prayer she wouldn't go ballistic on him.

Shaking her head, she laid a hand on his elbow and walked with a regal air through the door into the main hall with him.

"I need to do something special for you. A surprise, since you obviously like them. Oh, I know. I'm making you a big batch of brownies tomorrow. Just for you. With 'special' ingredients."

She leaned over and kissed his cheek, then whispered in his ear. "And you're going to eat them all."

Keil stopped them for a moment as they approached the center of the gathering. He stared into her eyes, watching as a twinkle of mischief overtook the anger.

She was amazing, this mate of his. Just what he needed in his life, and exactly what the pack needed as well.

He released her arm and faced her. Carefully crossing his hands over his heart he dipped his head. *"I love you, Robyn. Shall we go become Alpha?"*

"With you, anything."

"Good. You get to share the brownies."

THE CEREMONY WAS GOING FINE, if over-the-top, out-of-this-world-shifter rituals could be fine.

All the way up to where they'd done a little walk around the pack members, and recited a little ditty about being there for the wellbeing of the entire pack, she'd seen skepticism on a few faces.

She wasn't upset with the stragglers who still wondered if she truly were strong enough to do the job Keil had so boldly proclaimed was hers.

Robyn had spent a lifetime watching others, and examining the faces around them as she walked arm in arm with Keil was a final chance for her to decide if she truly wanted to do this.

Well, the mate thing with Mr. Sexy was a given, but the whole Alpha job hadn't been on her agenda a week ago.

Yet the longer she considered it, the more *right* this entire crazy situation felt. The hesitant few in the pack were far outnumbered by the accepting and the curious, and from all of them she sensed something that made her decision an easy one.

Connection. *Belonging.*

Even the wolves who were worried about the newcomer in their midst had accepted her as one of them—and as the ceremony continued, the layers of what that meant grew stronger and stronger.

Finally Keil led her to the front of the room, and they turned in unison toward the gathered crowd. Faces before her were tinged with a sense of *other*-ness that she now identified as their shifter part. Human and animal, and wholly unique.

Wholly hers. *Theirs.*

She tightened her grip on his fingers as she examined the pack closer. An eerie sense of knowledge drifted over her. *That woman*—she was worried about a job interview she had the following day. *That man*—he'd had to ground his teenage son, and now he was trying to think of ways to rebuild their relationship to be stronger, more supportive...

Every face told a story. Not their intimate secrets, although Robyn sensed she could dig deeper if she wanted to ferret them out. But the current joys and concerns of all their hearts were there to be witnessed, *and* she instinctively knew exactly how to help them get through to the next step.

Whoa. This gig was real.

The sky overhead cleared, a break in the clouds letting moonlight stream down. It landed in a near perfect circle not ten feet from where they stood. The light slowly moved toward them, like a spotlight highlighting the dais where wolfie royalty appeared in state before the commoners...

She snorted at the mental image. Um...*no.* She certainly didn't plan on being Queen Top Dog. Wolf. Whatever.

"*I'm glad you're enjoying yourself,*" Keil teased, voice stroking her mind.

She glanced at him, suddenly struck with more thoughts.

His—

Shared amusement. Caring. Times spent talking late into the night, working to make her happy. Building a family and building a life. Sex...

Whoops, that final thought packed a lot of power behind it, and she blushed. "*What comes next?*

He waggled his brows. "*You do.*"

Oh, no. That whole "sex in front of the pack" thing wasn't happening. Not on her watch.

Robyn opened her mouth to tell him that when the moonlight hit them and the world shifted ten feet to the left.

The light intensified. Shadows faded as her vision sharped. Scents grew thicker, stronger. Images danced into her head as she dragged air in through her nose.

What was that one? That delicious, distracting aroma?

She sniffed harder. Her skin twitched as she identified the animal, and instantly began plotting how soon she could track it down and—

"*Robyn.*" Keil's prod was full of amusement. "*We're kind of busy at the moment. Maybe you could leave off chasing bunnies for a few hours.*"

Oops.

She jerked her attention back to where they were, which was in a place that sparkled with light and texture. She lifted her arms in front of her to discover her skin shimmered with moonlight. Tingles slipped up and down her spine, and every breath felt intoxicating. "*Is this supposed to happen?*"

Keil stepped beside her, his eyes wide with admiration. "You're perfect."

She gazed back into his face where his love for her was written clear as day, and a sudden burst of surety struck.

Who knew if it was kosher, but she was doing it anyway.

Robyn lifted her arms. She signed, and spoke the words to him out loud, and inside his head. A triple-decker layer of honesty, sharing a promise she knew she could keep.

"You're *mine.* I'm yours. Today and forever. Together

we will be the best Alphas Granite Lake has ever seen. Not because we're physically strong—"

"—*but we totally are*," he silently interrupted with a wink.

She laughed then continued. "Because we'll work together, and every action will be built on the strongest thing there is."

"*Love.*"

The entire pack shouted the answer, and she and Keil fist bumped before turning to accept the pack's approval.

The cheering and arm shaking hadn't even died down when he caught her fingers in his and kissed her knuckles.

The tingles under her skin accelerated from intense to electrifying.

The next second magic took her. Whether it was biological or something out of this world, Robyn didn't know and didn't care. All she knew was as she stared into the eyes of the man she loved, reality flipped itself inside out. Her robe fell unminded to the ground as pleasure coursed through her veins and she...

...landed on four feet with Keil's perfect wolf standing opposite her.

Oh. My. Word.

Robyn shook herself, instinctively bracing her paws, breathing deep as she threw back her head and let loose the joy waiting to explode out of her.

She howled for all of two seconds before falling over in shock.

"*You okay?*" Keil asked, brushing his body past hers.

Was she okay? "*I heard me. I heard my howl.*"

His hip bumped her. "*Your wolf didn't have a fever, I guess. You might regret that at some point—wolves are damn noisy in their fur.*"

Nothing about being a wolf was up for regrets. She eyed her mate, and the gathering in front of them, some of whom had already shifted and were waiting anxiously. Her body felt powerful and wild, and the urge to run was impossible to ignore.

"*Hey, Keil,*" she whispered.

He stood in front of her, lowering his upper body slightly so he could stare into her eyes.

Robyn tightened her muscles, prepping herself for the right moment. "*You're it.*"

She exploded toward the exit, heading at a full sprint toward the trees where the wilderness scents and fresh, clean air beckoned.

Keil caught up with her moments later, and they ran.

Together.

EPILOGUE

*a*s he waited for Keil and Robyn and the others to return, Tad wrestled with mixed emotions.

He was so glad for his sister—it was clear she was finally exactly where she was supposed to be, and with the perfect man. Mates being what they were, there was no question of that.

And not that she'd ever really needed a protector, knowing Keil would always be there for her made it easier for Tad to step back out of worrying like he had for the past twenty plus years...

Okay, that was bull, because, he was still going to worry. She was family, and taking care of her was what he was supposed to do. Even when it was clear she was in a powerful new place in her life.

What he needed was a distraction. Something new to focus his energy and attention on.

Fortunately, or unfortunately, he knew exactly what thing he'd been fixated over for years. Ever since he'd discovered the truth about shifters—thank you, TJ, for being a clumsy fool—Tad had been trying to solve his own dilemma.

He wanted it. Bad.

Not just to be a wolf, although that haunted his dreams and made his very skin itch. He wanted it *all*. The mate, the pack, the *belonging*...and what he had now was a sort of drifting with the tide.

He had a pack, yes, but his place was uncertain. Not like Robyn, who was now the center of the Granite Lake universe with Keil at her side.

It wasn't jealousy, even. Hell, Tad didn't care if it turned out he was somewhere near the bottom of the pack, although he doubted it. It was the uncertainty that killed his joy every damn time.

And forget finding a mate. Forget getting to fool around within the pack, stupid half-breed hormones and freaking wolf sexual *woohoo*.

Sex. He straight up needed some.

Yup, while his troubles were far from over, that's what he needed to focus on with all the energy he now didn't need to spend on his sister.

Plotting to have a damn good time was better than moping. *Anything* was better than sitting and waiting for life to happen.

As he lifted a hand to acknowledge the Granite Lake Beta's wave, rising to his feet to see what Erik wanted, Tad knew where he was going to go look for a solution once he was out of there.

The arms of a beautiful woman was the perfect place to start.

BONUS VIGNETTE: TJ'S BIG ADVENTURE

The following is a vignette about the day when Tad Maxwell found out about shifters. I hope you enjoy this short trip into history with Tad and a few members of the Granite Lake pack.

~Viv

PART I

Kluane National Park, Yukon
Some years in the past...

The sun shone off the surface of the lake to reflect a million sparkling jewels back into his eyes. The bright blue summer sky stretched from mountain peak to mountain peak. Tad maneuvered his floatplane toward the portable dock visible along the north shore of the small lake. He took a deep breath and congratulated himself for being smart enough to find a job that got his butt out of an office and into some of the most beautiful country anywhere in the world.

Damn, he loved to fly.

He had just tucked the plane next to the dock, neat as can be, when he felt a solid clasp to his shoulder.

"Nice landing, hotshot, very nice."

Tad grinned as he slipped the lock on his door and hurried to open the passenger compartment and let out his clients. This was the second time he'd flown a private booking for the Alaskan based Maximum Exposure Adventures. The owner, Keil Lynus, was a monster of a man with the arms of a gladiator and the gentlest demeanor.

"Great set up, Keil," Tad said as he secured the tethering ropes fore and aft, tightening them to keep the massive floats next to the dock. He admired the tidy little log cabin at the edge of the lake, a small storage shed tucked behind it next to the trees. "We can unload the gear in stages, or we can organize ourselves into a bucket brigade and get everything off the plane all the way to the cabin, or wherever you want it. Your choice."

The dock swayed as Keil climbed down to stand next to Tad. "What do you think, Erik? I'm game for the brigade. I hate picking things up a dozen times."

Tad watched as Keil's business partner and best friend twisted his shoulders sideways to get through the door. If Keil was big, Erik was the Friendly Giant on steroids.

With lots of tattoos.

"Definitely the long carry, only I think you and I should be on land. We'll put things where we can find them. The last time we let your little brother store gear it became part of the lost Templar Treasure."

"Hey," TJ complained, "Can I help it I like to organize supplies in a logical manner and you yahoos don't?" He sat on the edge of the plane doorway and made a face at his older brother. "And I do mean *Yahoos* in the purest sense of the word."

Tad grinned at his passengers and took a deep breath of the crisp fresh air.

He had flown full time for three months now and he hoped for many more days like this. Regular clients who treated the wilderness like a precious gem. People who returned to the same places to change them for the better, not trash them to the ground.

Tad thrilled to think he was on his way to secure a living doing what he loved.

After TJ whacked his head on the doorframe for the third time Tad held out a hand to restrain him. "Do you want me to pass you the stuff? I'm not as tall as you, and if you slam into the frame much more you'll bend it out of shape. I charge extra for things like that."

TJ jumped down and rubbed a hand over his forehead. "Sounds great. It was hard to turn around in the back too, and I've smacked my funny bone so many times it's gone numb. Not quite as bad as when my arm fell asleep and Keil threw something at me, and I couldn't reach up in time to grab it. Damn near broke my nose."

Tad chuckled as TJ stumbled toward the end of the dock, his arms full with duffle bags of supplies. Whatever they fed those boys down in Haines, Alaska, made them grow pretty damn big. Even TJ stood taller than Tad, and he wasn't small at almost six feet.

Tad turned back to ready another load when he heard a distant splash followed by a shrill scream.

Winter or summer, the water was glacier fed and icy cold.

He leapt to the dock to help the boy, but Keil beat him there. "TJ, you're a bloody idiot. What the hell are you doing?"

He reached down and with one hand, hauled the boy up to stand dripping wet beside him.

"Oops. I don't know how it happened. I mean, one of the boards must be loose or something."

Keil rubbed his hands over his face, took a calming breath, then pointed to the cabin. "Go get changed, Mom will kill me if I let you catch another cold. Put the kettle on to boil." He took a few paces toward the plane before he paused. "TJ, did you fall in before or after you picked up a load of gear?"

TJ bit his lip, and took a slow step away from his brother. He spun around and ran for the cabin like the devil was after him.

"That's what I thought." Keil muttered. He shouted after his fleeing younger sibling, "You're lucky Mom likes you, brat! Or you'd be swimming with the polar bears right now!"

Tad tried to keep his face blank as Keil approached the plane to take over carrying gear.

Keil chuckled. "Don't worry, I won't kill him. He's better than he used to be, if you can believe it. Just wait, you ain't seen nothing. Hang around with us for very long, and you'll feel right at home in a nuthouse."

Tad passed down another load of gear, and a flash of contentment surged.

He wasn't sure why, but spending time with this group of kooks felt very, very good.

"TJ, why are you hiding by the storage shed?" Tad had wandered the entire camp to find the boy.

"Because I can't hide in the cabin, and if I hide on the dock, well, duh, people will see me."

Tad shook his head in disbelief. "Are you insane? Are you going out of your way to piss your brother off? I thought you had to make lunch or something."

TJ leant on the barrels stacked behind him. Large plastic containers with a tight seal to keep bears out of the supplies stood in a neat line along the side wall of the storage shed.

"I already made lunch. It's on the table." He took a cautious look around before he confided, "Actually, Mom made lunch at home and I just unwrapped it. Don't tell Keil. I hope to gain some brownie points here."

"You're a menace to yourself, aren't you?"

"Klutz of the first order, that's me. Only I do have my redeeming qualities. I'm very well read, I have excellent dental hygiene, and I never fart in public unless I mean it."

Tad stared around the mountainside with delight as TJ rambled on. What a beautiful place to bring clients to canoe and fish and—

"Shit!"

Tad glanced back to see the boy nudge one of the barrels out of line with its partners.

"Careful, kid."

TJ shifted his body weight to the side to avoid the barrel on his right. That put him into contact with the one on the left, and it slid off its base, wiggled a few times and fell in a direct path toward TJ.

The entire wall of barrels collapsed in chaotic fashion, coming to land in a haphazard pile, the loud crash echoing through the air.

Frantic with concern, Tad raced to where TJ was buried to pull him out, shouting for help over his shoulder. "Keil, Erik. I need you."

He spotted TJ's boot under the mess.

Several of the barrels had landed propped on each other, forming a pocket of space. With some luck TJ wouldn't be crushed beneath the heavy load.

"Hang on, TJ, we'll get you out of there."

Tad gave a gentle tug on the boot, to see if it might be

possible...and then he wasn't sure what he had planned to do. Because the boot came loose in his hand, a plain white sock clinging to the inside.

"What the—?"

The barrels rocked, and Tad stepped back for a second. Heavy footsteps approached, and he had just turned back to the pile when he heard it.

A long, drawn out wolf howl coming from under the barrels.

PART II

___

Keil rushed up behind him. "Where's TJ, as if I don't already know the answer?"

Tad's finger trembled as he pointed at the barrels.

Low curses escaped Keil's lips. "Awesome. Just awesome." He raised his voice to shout at his brother. "I'm going to kill you, TJ. I swear I'm going to—"

Another howl rose on the air, and Tad shivered. "If we pull the top barrel—"

"It's okay. Give me a minute."

Keil stomped around to the backside of the pile and shoved hard. The rest of the pile shifted, and Tad tripped over his own feet in an attempt to reach safety and still keep his gaze on Keil.

A large shape slipped past the barrel.

An extra-large silver-grey timber wolf.

"Holy shit!" In a flash, Tad scrambled to his feet and fled from the wolf toward the safety of the shed door.

Keil blocked his path, standing with his hands up, open palms, "Hey, it's okay. Relax."

Tad fumbled with his belt, grabbing his hunting blade to hold it between them. "Relax? Shit, *shit*... no fucking way. What the hell is going on, Keil? Where's TJ?"

"Tad. Put the knife away. TJ's fine, he's right there behind the shed."

Tad flicked a glance sideways before pointing the knife back at Keil.

"He's a fucking wolf?"

Keil took a step back then crossed his arms. "Will you put the damn knife away so I can talk to you?"

"Not bloody likely."

"Tad, I'm warning you."

"No."

Keil reached under his padded vest and pulled out a handgun. Without a word he adjusted his stance, aiming straight at the center of Tad's chest.

They stood motionless, the sound of spring songbirds obscenely loud in the air around them, until Tad stood down and sheathed his knife.

"Damn American gun laws," he muttered.

The other man shrugged as he slipped away his pistol. "I've got a permit. I can't help it if you Canadians are too polite to carry."

"I have a shotgun in the plane," Tad said shortly.

"And I'm sure it'll come in real handy when the bears try to climb in for a free ride." Keil turned back to the storage area. "TJ," he ordered, "Get your furry ass out here now!"

The large silver grey wolf slunk around the corner, head dropped.

Keil motioned for Tad to join him. "I'd say all the usual

things like he's not going to hurt you, and don't panic, but saying it won't make this any easier." He pointed at the wolf where it sat on its haunches in front of them. "Tad, you've met TJ, otherwise known as Mr. Disaster. You may as well get a proper look."

"Look at wh—?"

"Shift, TJ," Keil commanded.

Tad swung his head back to stare at... *TJ*? Impossible.

For a moment the wolf regarded him with bright eyes before Tad's vision blurred, and instead of a large animal, there was a tall youth sitting buck-naked on the ground.

"I suppose it was too much trouble for you to ask me to shift once I was somewhere near clean clothes, hmmm?" TJ complained.

Keil glared at him.

TJ shut his mouth tight, biting his bottom lip hard.

His brother snapped up a hand, pointing toward the cabin, and for the second time in an hour TJ sprinted away from them.

Of course, this time he was naked, but Tad was trying real hard not to notice.

"Well, sorry for the sudden introduction to our reality, but... Hey, here we are," Keil announced.

"I'm actually in a coma somewhere, right? This is a dream, and I've got some freaky obsession with seeing TJ's ass."

Keil snorted. "I hope not. His ass is too young for you, even if you swung that way, which I don't think you do." He slapped a hand down on Tad's shoulder, tugging him toward the cabin. "Come on, I think you could use a little shot of bracer. We'll have some lunch, answer your questions. It'll work out fine."

Tad looked back over the lake again. Sun was still

shining; sky was still bright. Only in the past five minutes the whole world had flipped upside down.

Strange how quick life could change.

~

They pulled chairs onto the porch of the cabin so they could sit in the sun while they talked.

Tad threw back the shot of whatever it was Erik had handed him with no hesitation. If they wanted him dead they wouldn't have to waste time drugging his food or drink, and for some reason he was absolutely starving.

Apparently finding out that werewolves existed had that effect on his system.

"So... you're werewolves, but you don't need a full moon to change, and you're not into ripping people's throats open. I'm kinda glad about that particular detail."

"Mine." Keil snagged the last sandwich from the tray, slapping TJ's hand from it. "You're not very high in my good books right now, little bro. Go find something productive to do, like fishing out the gear bags you dropped off the dock."

TJ scrambled away.

"He's a natural disaster, but I do love him." Keil admitted.

Tad dragged a hand through his hair. "Okay dokey, since you're explaining yourself to me, what now? I have to swear some secret oaths to never reveal your presence? I'm sure this is all pretty hush-hush stuff, and I'm not supposed to know about you."

"Oh, no," Erik offered. "It's just fine for wolves to know about other wolves."

Tad froze. "What...are you talking about?"

"You smell like a wolf, Tad," Erik said.

"But it's not full strength. Probably one of your parents, or maybe one of your grandparents is a wolf. You're what we'd call a half breed, no matter how many generations back the wolf is in your family tree," Keil informed him.

"You're shitting me. I've never turned into a wolf."

"No, you won't be able to until you get the wolf genes turned on. You need a special hormone to flip the switch, so to speak." Keil stared at him, his face unreadable.

Holy shit.

Tad sat there quietly, watching the other men as he tried to wrap his brain around the impossible. "So, why has no one told me this? Like my folks, or Grampa, or whoever?"

"There's no way for us to know," Keil said. "It's possible your gene donor was an outcast and didn't want to tell you. As for anyone else mentioning it, well, full-bloods don't tend to tell half-bloods who aren't aware of their heritage because... Well, I have to confess it's a bit of a race bias thing. I don't really hold with that way of thinking. Erik and I had discussed if we should tell you. You know, after we met you last trip."

He looked guilty enough that Tad felt a little better about the secret keeping. Keil and Erik were good guys overall. Other than the going furry and pointing guns at people bit.

Erik nodded. "The real point is you've got the blood, and if you get triggered, you'll be able to shift."

Oh, man. Getting to be a wolf? How awesome would that be?

"Wow. So how do I get the hormone? I'd love to be able to turn into a wolf." Tad leaned closer, trying to decipher Keil and Erik's suddenly strange expressions.

"Does it cost a lot? Because I've got *some* money saved up—"

"It's not money you need. It's..." Erik shrugged. "It's... complicated. Simple, but complicated."

Keil broke in, speaking firmly. "And that's all we're going to say right now."

"No damn way," Tad all but shouted. "That's not fair. I don't care how complicated it is, you've got to tell me. I mean, you've already sprung the 'There are werewolves living amongst us' card, and the 'You are one of us' card. This last thing can't be any worse. Spit it out, you bastard."

Erik grimaced, tucking himself protectively between Tad and Keil, although it seemed he was protecting Tad from Keil. "Umm, slow down there, junior. One thing you'll eventually learn is wolves don't like being ordered around. Especially not Alpha wolves."

Gabbly-gook. This was bullshit. "Well, tough cookies. *I* find it hard not to be pissed off when people—excuse me, *wolves*—refuse to tell me what I need to know."

"It's not my place," Keil snapped. "You live in Whitehorse. You have to talk to the Alpha there, or we could start a territorial war."

"And as much as we like you," Erik offered, "we try to avoid death and dying on principle, when possible."

Tad's stomach rolled. This was too bizarre. Werewolves had rules that would make a person's head spin.

He picked up the flashlight next to him, flicking it off and on rapidly. "So much for me thinking you were some of the good guys..."

"I *am* being good. You have no idea what you're about to step into." Keil grabbed the flashlight from Tad. "Stop that, it's annoying me."

"That makes us even, because you're annoying *me*."

Tad ignored the growling noise escaping the other man. His give-a-shit-meter seemed to be broken. Instead he glanced at his watch. "Fine. I've got to be going soon if I'm going to make it back to the airstrip before my deadline. Are you sure TJ is all right, or should I fly him out?"

Erik shook his head. "Wolves have really good healing powers. I bet he's only got a few bruises left by now."

Tad gave a brisk nod before turning to the...*Alpha*? wolf who was his friend. Or had been until now. "Keil. Fine, I'll trust you on this one. Set up a meeting with the other groups, or pack, or whatever I need to get comfortable with. All right?"

Keil stuck out his hand and shook Tad's firmly. "You're a good man, Tad."

"Yeah, well I appreciate you, you know, not ripping out my throat, or shooting me or something when I found out your secret."

Erik laughed. "It's much neater this way. Having to clean blood off Gore-Tex is a pain in the ass."

"I'll call the packs around Whitehorse. Someone will make contact so they can teach you what you need to know, and how to settle in. Because, Tad," Keil looked him in the eye, "You *are* a wolf. You need to be with pack mates to be really happy. Don't deny that part of yourself."

Tad nodded and swung his daypack onto his back, walking firmly back to his plane.

Werewolves. Who would have thought?

～

New York Times Bestselling Author Vivian Arend
brings you a series of light-hearted,
stand-alone novellas, with fated mates and always a
happily-ever-after.

～

Granite Lake Wolves
Wolf Signs
Wolf Flight
Wolf Games
Wolf Tracks
Wolf Line
Wolf Nip

～

ABOUT THE AUTHOR

New York Times and *USA Today* bestselling author Vivian Arend loves to share the products of her over-active imagination with her readers. She writes contemporary, western, and light-hearted paranormal romances. The stories are humorous yet emotional, usually with a large cast of family or friends, and a guaranteed happily-ever-after.

Vivian lives in British Columbia, Canada, with her husband of many years—her inspiration for every hero and a willing companion for all sorts of adventures.

Find out more at www.vivianarend.com.

Made in the USA
Las Vegas, NV
09 December 2021

36745402R00083